SAUCY

ALSO BY CYNTHIA KADOHATA

Checked

Cracker! The Best Dog in Vietnam

Half a World Away

Kira-Kira

A Million Shades of Gray

Outside Beauty

A Place to Belong

The Thing About Luck

Weedflower

CYNTHIA KADOHATA

SAUCY

Illustrated by Marianna Raskin

A CAITLYN DLOUHY BOOK

Atheneum Books for Young Readers

New York   London   Toronto   Sydney   New Delhi

A
atheneum

Atheneum Books for Young Readers
An imprint of Simon & Schuster Children's Publishing Division
1230 Avenue of the Americas, New York, New York 10020
This book is a work of fiction. Any references to historical events, real people, or real places are used fictitiously. Other names, characters, places, and events are products of the author's imagination, and any resemblance to actual events or places or persons, living or dead, is entirely coincidental.
Text © 2020 by Cynthia Kadohata
Cover illustration © 2020 by Marianna Raskin
Cover design by Lauren Rille © 2020 by Simon & Schuster, Inc.
Interior illustration © 2020 by Marianna Raskin
All rights reserved, including the right of reproduction in whole or in part in any form.
ATHENEUM BOOKS FOR YOUNG READERS is a registered trademark of Simon & Schuster, Inc. Atheneum logo is a trademark of Simon & Schuster, Inc.
For information about special discounts for bulk purchases, please contact Simon & Schuster Special Sales at 1-866-506-1949 or business@simonandschuster.com.
The Simon & Schuster Speakers Bureau can bring authors to your live event. For more information or to book an event, contact the Simon & Schuster Speakers Bureau at 1-866-248-3049 or visit our website at www.simonspeakers.com.
Also available in an Atheneum Books for Young Readers hardcover edition
Interior design by Lauren Rille
The text for this book was set in Meridien.
The illustrations for this book were digitally rendered.
0821 OFF
First Atheneum Books for Young Readers paperback edition September 2021
10 9 8 7 6 5 4 3 2 1
The Library of Congress has cataloged the hardcover edition as follows:
Names: Kadohata, Cynthia, author. | Raskin, Marianna, illustrator.
Title: Saucy / Cynthia Kadohata ; illustrated by Marianna Raskin.
Description: First edition. | New York : Atheneum Books for Young Readers, [2020] | Audience: Ages 8–12. | Audience: Grades 4–6. | Summary: When eleven-year-old Becca, a quadruplet, finds a sick piglet on the side of the road, her life is changed forever.
Identifiers: LCCN 2020009952 | ISBN 9781442412781 (hardcover) | ISBN 9781442412798 (pbk) | ISBN 9781442412804 (eBook)
Subjects: CYAC: Animal rescue—Fiction. | Pigs—Fiction. | Animals—Infancy—Fiction. | Quadruplets—Fiction. | Brothers and sisters—Fiction. | Family life—Fiction. | Friendship—Fiction.
Classification: LCC PZ7.K1166 Sau 2020 | DDC [Fic]—dc23
LC record available at https://lccn.loc.gov/2020009952

FOR CAITLYN DLOUHY
& JUSTIN CHANDA

CONTENTS

CHAPTER ONE · 1
SUMMER

CHAPTER TWO · 11
ON BEING A COWARD

CHAPTER THREE · 20
WALKING

CHAPTER FOUR · 29
AN ARMADILLO, MAYBE

CHAPTER FIVE · 42
SAUCY

CHAPTER SIX · 50
A *VERY* SICK PIG

CHAPTER SEVEN · 54
GEEZ!

CHAPTER EIGHT · 62
TRACKS ANIMAL HOSPITAL

CHAPTER NINE • 74
PERFECT

CHAPTER TEN • 92
PIG-AMONIUM

CHAPTER ELEVEN • 106
BATHTIME

CHAPTER TWELVE • 111
THE LIST

CHAPTER THIRTEEN • 121
THE KITCHEN FLOOR

CHAPTER FOURTEEN • 129
SAUCY GOES FOR A WALK

CHAPTER FIFTEEN • 134
SHINER

CHAPTER SIXTEEN • 141
SIT, STAY, COME!

CHAPTER SEVENTEEN • 147
CRISPY

CHAPTER EIGHTEEN • 153
A GOOD LIFE

CHAPTER NINETEEN • 174
GAINING WEIGHT

CHAPTER TWENTY • 179
THE LAST WALK

CHAPTER TWENTY-ONE • 192
SANCTUARY

CHAPTER TWENTY-TWO • 210
FORTY-NINE THINGS

CHAPTER TWENTY-THREE • 219
HOW SAUCY LIVED

CHAPTER TWENTY-FOUR • 228
THE FACTORY FARM

CHAPTER TWENTY-FIVE • 249
A MOMENT OF PEACE

CHAPTER TWENTY-SIX • 252
HOUSE OF PIGS

CHAPTER TWENTY-SEVEN • 262
THE MEETING

CHAPTER TWENTY-EIGHT • 275
TRANSCENDING

CHAPTER ONE
SUMMER

Becca sat in the backyard, trying to meditate. She had decided that meditation would be her thing, the thing she was better at than everybody else—if it was even possible to be a "better" meditator. Like wasn't meditation kind of the same as doing nothing, and how could you get better at that than other people? Regardless, she was going to get very good at it.

It was a little noisy to be meditating, though.

One problem was that every few seconds Jammer whacked one of his one hundred hockey pucks into the goal. Becca didn't understand how he could be interested in doing the exact same thing, over and over. Like if you did it perfectly one time, why did you need to keep doing it?

Bailey was drumming his fingers on the arm of his wheelchair, mouthing words and nodding to an imaginary song playing in his head. Bailey could turn on music in his mind just like other people could turn on music on their phones. He also wrote songs, and you weren't allowed to say anything at all to him while he was writing or singing. Like now.

K.C., sitting right next to Becca, was reading a book about physics. Becca supposed that he was a math and science genius. Everybody said so, anyway. Even though to her he just seemed like K.C. She didn't understand half of what he said. Nobody did. Becca could feel his arm against hers. Even when he was reading something and completely in his own world, he always did this thing of sitting close to somebody else—he didn't really care who.

Mom had bought Becca a special meditation cushion called a zafu that was soft but not too soft. It was really pretty, with a picture of the moon and stars, but since her butt was on it, she wasn't sure why it mattered how pretty it was. Still, she closed her eyes and tried to focus. But the only thing she could think about was the little ache in her heart that seemed to be there, like *all the time*.

Becca and her brothers were quadruplets. She was born first, on December 26, at 12:01 a.m. Then came Jammer. He was supposedly the quietest baby. Even today, he hardly talked to anyone, because they were all so boring. If you didn't play hockey like he did, then you were boring. He was born at 12:03. Then K.C. at 12:05. That was when Dad passed out, so he didn't see Bailey get born at 12:06. Becca had heard the story of Dad passing out at least a million times. Who wouldn't pass out? he liked to say.

But *ugh*. Becca couldn't concentrate! She opened her left eye. Bailey was dancing in his wheelchair, a new dance she hadn't seen before. It must have been a good song he was hearing in his head, because the dance was really cool.

"That dance is dope," K.C. said, looking up now. "It's so perfect, it reminds me of a robot." That was a compliment, because K.C. thought robots were the greatest thing ever, or would be someday. Becca closed her eye again and tried to concentrate but still couldn't.

She hummed her mantra, which was a word or phrase to help you meditate. Hers was simply "Ommmm." She'd chosen this one because it was simple and because it supposedly was the vibration of the universe . . . whatever that meant— she couldn't quite remember at the moment. But anyway, the definition of "om" was "it is."

"I can't concentrate when you're doing that," Jammer snapped.

"I can't concentrate when you're doing *that*," she snapped back.

Then they both returned to what they'd been doing.

Eleven and a half years ago, Becca, Bailey, Jammer, and K.C. had been in the intensive care unit for a month. Either Mom, Dad, Grandma, or Grandpa was at the hospital every second. Dad said it might sound weird, but even though he and Mom weren't allowed to even pick up their "quads" for the first few days, that was the most magical time of his life. He and Mom hadn't thought they could have kids at all, and being able to go to the hospital and see those "four tiny, precious creatures" was like "a new lease on life" and "being on cloud nine." That was the way Dad talked sometimes. He said the reason clichés like "a new lease on life" and "being on cloud nine" existed was because they were so often the exact right words to say. That wasn't what Becca's last teacher believed, though. If you used a cliché in your stories, she would slash through it and write *CLICHÉ ALERT* in the margin. Which was really annoying, to be honest.

And suddenly Becca was thinking about how annoying that was, and she absolutely couldn't meditate even slightly.

"I can't focus," she announced. "K.C., how do I empty my head?" Even though K.C. thought about the world *a lot*, he could also empty his head whenever he wanted. He said so, anyway.

"Maybe somebody is stopping you from focusing, just for fun," he explained patiently.

That made no sense, but Becca asked, "Like who?"

He shrugged. "It could be anybody."

K.C. believed that they might all be living in a simulation, being controlled by someone or something. He had read how some techie recently said that when he worked on artificial intelligence, he felt like he was operating on alien—not human—technology. Even though *humans* had invented AI. In short, this simulation on earth was possibly being run by an extremely advanced AI program that was invented by a flesh-and-blood alien a billion years ago, and the inventor had already died. According to K.C.

Whatever, K.C. That was what Becca thought when he talked about that kind of stuff. She tried to listen politely, except when it was late and he wouldn't shut up and let her or Jammer or Bailey sleep. Then she would actually say "shut up" out loud. It was okay to tell K.C. "shut up" because he never got offended and would just say "shut up yourself." But you could never, ever tell Bailey to shut up, because he would cry. And you didn't usually have to tell Jammer to shut up, because people didn't talk to him much, on account of they didn't want to bore him, and he didn't talk to them, on account of they were boring. She had to admit he was a really, really good hockey player, though. It was almost as cool as Bailey's dancing. Actually, maybe just as cool.

Still, she suddenly felt annoyed again. Trying to meditate was *annoying*. So she called out, "Jammer, would you *please* mind being quiet for a few minutes so I can meditate?"

"It's a free world," he said, whacking a new puck.

"You're so annoying!" she said. But he didn't answer. Naturally.

She pulled her pillow out from under her butt. It wasn't helping her meditate at all. She wondered if Mom could get her money back for it.

Then, as soon as she thought that, she felt calm, like maybe she could meditate now. So she sat on her zafu again and tried to empty her head. But she couldn't.

It was all right, though. In fact, she would never admit it to Jammer, but she kind of liked hearing the pucks whack. She liked hearing Bailey sing. She liked K.C.'s arm bumping hers.

They all spent a lot of time together. She knew other multiples who were like, *meh, being a multiple is no big deal*. But sometimes, at least when nobody was fighting, Becca felt she and her brothers were as connected now as when they were still in their mom's stomach. Being a multiple was probably the thing in the world she was secretly most grateful for.

But she had questions. Like why were her brothers all so *focused*? They were nice enough people, but they were like *sharks* for what they liked. She was more like a jellyfish. Just floating around here and there.

Trying to meditate.

And failing.

CHAPTER TWO
ON BEING A COWARD

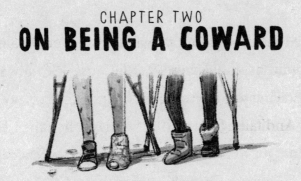

Okay, she knew one reason she couldn't focus. It was because she had that little ache in her heart. This ache had to do with a bad thing she had done to MacKenzie Fulton. A few months ago, before she moved, MacKenzie was the actual nicest girl in their grade, maybe even the nicest girl ever. She'd been Becca's friend since they were eight. They had broken their big toes the same year. (Becca tripped in the snow; MacKenzie's foot got run over by a skateboard.) They had gotten the same haircut for two years straight—it came exactly two inches below their shoulders. They had binge-watched *The Walking Dead* until it got boring.

Even though Becca was only eleven, she got to watch *The Walking Dead* because K.C. always got to watch anything he wanted, since nothing bothered him, and it wouldn't be fair if she didn't get to as well. Jammer hardly watched TV at all, because it was so boring, and Bailey was too sensitive to watch just about anything. When *The Walking Dead* had gotten too gory, Becca and MacKenzie had screamed and turned their heads away. That was fun.

And right before they stopped being friends late last fall, they'd had the best sleepover ever. Becca was staying over at MacKenzie's, and MacKenzie got the idea that they should go out for a walk, even though it was still really early out. This seemed like a thrilling idea! So they snuck out in their pajamas, wrapped in blankets, and walked to the house of a boy they knew and started throwing pebbles at his window. His name was Nic, and he had no friends. That was why they chose him to come out with them, like in case he was lonely. Nic climbed out his window in *his* pajamas, and then they went to another girl's house and threw pebbles at her window, but the girl's mom came out in a robe and yelled at them. So the three of them walked down the quiet, empty road, feeling so *free* in the dark, empty world that they had never been outside in this late before. Nic had a look of pure happiness on his face, like he could hardly believe he was hanging around in the middle of the night with two *girls*. At one point, a car with a blaring radio drove by, and they got scared for no reason that the driver might kill them, and they ran as fast as they could and hid in some trees. The car braked with a slight screech, and they were sure they were going to be killed, even though probably the driver was just wondering why three kids were running around in the middle of the night. But then the car drove on.

Finally MacKenzie had said, "It's gone."

"But what if it comes back?" Becca had asked.

So they waited a few more minutes before starting their walk again. The feeling of *free* came flooding back. Becca imagined it was like how birds or foxes or something else wild felt, all the time. Like they could do *anything* and go *anywhere*.

Then MacKenzie checked her phone and said, "Uh-oh, my parents will wake up soon! We'll get in trouble!"

As they headed back home, Nic split off at his street and jogged away, calling out, "Bye! You can wake me up again if you want!"

But they never did. Because a few days later, MacKenzie's mom got *arrested*, though Becca had no idea why. She got put in *jail*. Just like that.

Even though she had just cooked pancakes for them three days earlier. Even though everything had seemed fine. Becca had thought Mrs. Fulton was just a regular mom. And yet, a few weeks later, she did this thing called "pleading guilty," and after that was when she got locked up.

It wasn't MacKenzie who'd been arrested! It wasn't MacKenzie who'd pled guilty! Yet everybody at school had turned on MacKenzie so swiftly and so completely that Becca understood that she herself must drop MacKenzie as a friend, or everyone would turn on *her*. That is, they didn't turn on Mac exactly. She became a nonperson; nobody even noticed she was there anymore. And Becca had not wanted to become a nonperson too. So she ignored Mac, just like everybody else did. She had felt so guilty that she secretly cried in bed at night.

Probably, MacKenzie was crying herself to

sleep at night as
well, a lot harder
than Becca was. Becca
was pretty sure about this,
and it made her cry even more.
Even Nic wouldn't talk to MacKenzie. It
was true he didn't have friends, but at least
people acknowledged him. Becca saw him avert
his eyes from Mac's as they passed in the hallway.
Just like she herself averted her eyes every time
she felt MacKenzie look at her.

One night Bailey had suddenly said to Becca,
"We hear you crying, you know. All the time. We
know why you're crying too."

"I don't want to talk about it!"

"I know. You can if you want, though. We'll listen." He went quiet, then added, "Well, good night, Beccers."

"Good night, Bai."

About five months later, MacKenzie's mom had gotten out of jail, and the entire family moved away.

Before she left, MacKenzie had rung their doorbell and asked Mom if she could speak with Becca. So Becca stepped outside, and they talked on the top of the steps.

"I'm moving to Indiana," MacKenzie had said, looking at Becca's face expectantly. Expecting what, though?

Becca looked down at her feet, then looked up and decided to say an honest thing. "I was scared to stay friends with you. I'm really sorry."

Then they cried and hugged, and MacKenzie left.

Maybe if Becca had stood by MacKenzie, they wouldn't have had to move away. It was shocking to think that she herself as an eleven-year-old maybe could have changed whether an entire family had to move away or not. And ever since, Becca knew that there was something inside of her that was bad, and cowardly.

But she had questions. For instance, did *everybody* have a bad, cowardly side to them? Or only a few horrible people like her?

Regardless, the fact was that she was a coward. This was her biggest secret. It was a lonely, sad secret to know about yourself, and she wished she could forget it. Or become brave.

CHAPTER THREE
WALKING

One evening Becca's whole family was out walking together, as they usually did each night, even when there was rain or snow. It was July, and their small Ohio town had been hot and humid all day. Their town was kind of—how to explain it? Kind of like Becca, actually: ordinary. Not full of rich people, and not full of poor people. Not country and not city and not suburb. There were some farms at the outskirts, and a couple of closed factories, but she honestly didn't know what most people did for a living.

Grandma was making this commotion the way she did once in a while, where she would

sniff loudly and shake her head at the same time. Mom had said it was just a tic, and to ignore it. Dad had said Grandma didn't have any tics at all when he was a boy. She was quite normal then, he'd said, which was actually rather hard for Becca to imagine.

Bailey was on the side of the road, ahead of them all. He had a motorized wheelchair that he'd gotten just a few months ago. Becca had heard her parents discussing how the "insurance" would pay for most of it—it cost $15,000!—or was thinking about paying for it, or something. She didn't know who or what exactly the "insurance" was, but it was nice of them to pay for part of it. If they had.

Her brother started zigzagging, the flashing green lights on the back of the chair moving left and right in a way that almost made Becca dizzy. This was an extremely excellent wheelchair, and

Bailey loved it a lot. Sometimes, for no reason, he whooped loudly, just because this wheelchair was so much more excellent than his previous one. He could go over bumps and grass, and he even went down a curb once with no problem. "Oh, yeah!" he cried out now. "Oh, yeah!"

Grandma stopped her sniffing and squinted at him. "It's not a toy, young man!" she rebuked him. She rebuked and scolded and reprimanded all of them for things that in Becca's opinion were not worth rebuking a person over. She even did it to Mom and Dad sometimes. Also, they had gotten pulled over by a police officer once, and Grandma scolded him for daring to pull over a nice family like theirs when there were criminals on the streets. She scolded a cashier at the grocery store for having to look up the code for oranges, and she scolded a man walking his well-behaved dog without a leash across the street. Basically, if you crossed her path for any reason at all, she might scold you. And if you lived with her, well, she might scold you at any time, even if you were just sitting on the couch looking at your phone.

She turned suddenly to Becca and said, "Why are you wearing flip-flops instead of tennis shoes?"

"Because I like my toes to breathe—it's hot out," Becca explained.

Then Grandma scolded Mom and Dad for letting her wear flip-flops, because a piece of glass might somehow get under her foot, and she would need stitches, and her cut might get infected and it would be a disaster. "I needed fifteen stitches once when I stepped on a piece of glass," Grandma said, as if this proved her point about flip-flops. Which it didn't, because Grandma had been barefoot when she stepped on the glass.

They were passing the big, empty building that used to be a factory, but it had closed, as had lots of other factories in this part of Ohio. Dad said thousands of factories had closed in the last few decades. Some had opened up, too, but not nearly as many as had closed. The way their family had ended up in Ohio was that Mom was part Japanese, and during World War II, Becca's great-grandma had come here from Arizona to help with the war effort by working in a canning factory, the factory that was closed now and that they were now walking by. Then Great-Grandma's mother stayed in Ohio because she met a young man with green eyes at the factory. That was why Becca's eyes were green, even though her parents and brothers had brown eyes.

They had reached the edge of town. Mom was humming as she strolled. Out of tune, because that was the way she hummed. It kind of bothered

Becca sometimes how out of tune she got, but Becca never said anything, because except for being totally unmusical, she was a really, really good mom.

She was the household scheduler, so she was super busy. Basically, their entire regular schedule for each week revolved around (1) Bailey's physical therapy for his CP, or cerebral palsy, and (1) Jammer's hockey needs, which were mostly thirty miles in the opposite direction from the office where Dad was an accountant. There was no 2. Just two number 1's. Usually. Bailey's needs were the actual most important thing, like in the entire world, but in terms of daily life, Jammer's needs took up just as much time. Probably more. Becca tried to take up no time. Just because she didn't want to bother anyone too much.

Mom had stopped humming, which was a

good thing, and she and Dad were walking next to each other, talking softly, sometimes laughing. Dad was six foot two and kind of thin, except for his stomach, and Mom was five foot two and kind of thin, except for *her* stomach. Dad had what Jammer called "flat, boring hair," which was a thing a lot of the local hockey boys tried to avoid. Hockey boys thought about their hair excessively, in Becca's opinion.

But now they all had to stop because K.C. had paused, gazing at the sky, pulling at his own hair so that it went *poof* on top like he was a mad scientist. He was probably looking for glitches, like a star "out of place." He actually studied star charts to see if something was ever somewhere it shouldn't be. If it was, that would absolutely prove the simulation . . . supposedly . . . Becca had heard him say so many times. Anyway, he started walking again, so apparently the stars were in the right places, as they always were every single time he looked.

They reached the place Becca didn't like, a beautiful stretch with bushes and trees and wild vines everywhere you looked. It was the kind of place that was so pretty it almost scared you. Like, just full of nature. Back when Becca and MacKenzie used to ride their bikes here, the air was full of butterflies and birds, and everything was green. But for some reason, this stretch of road gave Becca the faintest clammy feeling, as if, well, as if a demon had passed at one point, or somebody had been buried there. That is, no imminent danger, just like something wasn't right, or had been wrong at some point. She had never mentioned it to anyone, but she felt it— every single time.

CHAPTER FOUR

AN ARMADILLO, MAYBE

Grandma was complaining. "Someone needs to get me a wheelchair just like Bailey's. But nobody cares about me."

They for sure didn't have enough money to get Grandma a wheelchair like Bailey had. After they'd first decided to get it in January, and even though they didn't even *have* it yet, Jammer hadn't been allowed to buy new skates despite how squished his toes were. Then her parents got their "tax refund" in May, and they could afford the new skates. A "tax refund" was where you got a check in the mail, for some reason. It was a good thing!

Becca never asked for anything that cost a lot of money, because she was saving up imaginary credit for someday when she *really* wanted something. Also because she was just Becca. Her zafu had cost $29.99, and before that Becca couldn't even remember the last special thing she'd gotten.

Anyway. At the moment Grandma was groaning dramatically. "I'm getting tired! Is anyone listening to me?!" She groaned again. Extremely dramatic, like she might actually be dying. "Why do we even go on these walks?" She pressed her palms on her head as if she were holding her brains in.

But Becca figured that Grandma's brain was fine. Because Grandma suddenly smiled slightly, like she was only trolling them with her complaining. Which for sure she was.

But just beyond Grandma, something caught

Becca's eye: a movement in a dense row of tall bushes and vines.

"Did anybody see that?" she asked, pointing to the right.

"What did you see *this* time?" Grandma said irritably, as if Becca asked this same question every night. Even though Becca couldn't remember a single other time she'd ever asked anybody that.

"I'm going to go look!" She crept near the bushes, getting a weird rushing feeling, like in her veins, as she knelt down. She could hear something. Whimpering? Or more like—soft squealing? She pushed aside some branches.

And there! Oh. My. Gosh. It was . . . a baby *armadillo*! Lying on its side, gazing at her. She had to admit she wasn't sure what a baby armadillo looked like, but it probably looked exactly like this.

"What is it?" Dad asked, coming over.

"An armadillo! It's alive! It's looking at me!"
Then it wasn't—looking at her, that is. Now it
looked—dead? Becca leaned closer, which made
the armadillo's eye suddenly open wider.

She leaned closer still. Its skin looked like
dry, cracked mud. Then, after a moment, she
announced, "Actually, it's a baby pig . . . *probably*,
it's a pig. *Maybe* it's a pig! It's covered in dry mud—
possibly it almost . . . drowned in quicksand!"

K.C. knelt beside her as Jammer said scorn-
fully, "Quicksand in Ohio?"

Dad peered over Becca's shoulder with his
phone's light on. "It's definitely, probably a piglet," he said. "It *could* be an armadillo, but I believe
it's a pig."

"Whatever it is, I can smell it from here,"
Bailey said.

"Do you think it's alive?" K.C. asked. Then

he looked around suspiciously. "This is a very unusual occurrence." Simulation-wise, he probably meant.

"It moved," Becca said. "I saw it move!" But then she wasn't sure it *had* moved. Yet, on the other hand, yes, it had *so* moved, because that was what had caught her attention in the first place.

"I've got a skate at six in the morning," Jammer called out. "So, let's either take it with us or leave it, but I gotta get back."

Becca had not even considered taking it with them! But now she realized they absolutely *had* to!

"Bec, it hasn't moved," K.C. was saying. He picked up a stick as if to poke at the tiny pig.

Becca grabbed his arm fiercely. "Don't touch my pig!"

"*Your* pig?"

"Sadly, I think its time on this earth has come and gone," Dad said solemnly, resting a hand on Becca's shoulder.

"I wanna see!" Bailey cried out. He motored over as the others moved aside.

Becca moved over too, but just a little. She was going to protect this piglike thing! She tried to sound dangerous as she shouted, "Nobody touch it!" Then when K.C. raised the stick again anyway, she growled like a *gangster*, "K.C., if you poke that pig, I'll stab *you* with a stick." Nobody reacted; they all knew she would do no such thing.

"It's dead, Bec," K.C. insisted.

Bailey stared for a moment before he disagreed. "No, it's not. It's alive. But I don't think it's a pig."

They all gathered around again. True, it had no hair. Becca had never seen a pig up close, but she knew they had hair.

And suddenly the maybe-pig had a convulsion, its whole body shaking violently.

Becca abruptly burst into tears. She whipped around to her parents. "Do something!" She whipped back around to the animal. It was so little!

Mom was saying, "I don't know what we could do. The poor thing looks half-dead."

Becca kept crying, the tears pouring out. She did not want this armadillo-pig to die!

Dad knelt. "Well . . . should we take it with us?"

"I don't have time to take care of an animal, whatever it is," Mom said. She was always thinking about how much time she didn't have.

"Mom, I promise, I'll take care of it," Becca begged. She hoped Mom didn't remember when Becca had promised to take care of a flower garden last summer if they bought her seeds, and then she never took care of it, and every plant in her garden died.

"It's mange," Jammer announced out of the blue. "It's a pig with mange."

Becca considered this. Jammer usually didn't know anything about anything except hockey. But sometimes he surprised everybody.

He took two steps back. "If it's sarcoptic mange, it's super contagious. Humans can get it."

Everybody—even Becca—immediately moved backward.

Then Becca shined her own phone light on the armadillo-pig. It was the saddest, most pathetic thing she had ever seen. The mange, if that's what it truly was, covered most of its body, like the thick, cracked bark of the oak tree in their backyard.

Becca looked pleadingly at her parents. "We can't let it die!" She hesitated. "Please, can we at least take it to the animal hospital? Pleeeeeeeease? We can find something to wrap it up with so we won't get mange!" She looked desperately around, her eyes falling on . . . Dad's shirt! "Dad! Can we use your shirt? Pleeeeeeease?"

"Ahhhhhh!" Grandma said. "It's hideous. Don't touch it, Jason, I'm warning you! *I'm commanding you!*"

Becca fell to her knees and clasped her hands together. "Dad, I'm begging you!" Still on her knees, she turned to her mother. "Mom!" She felt dizzy with desperation. "We need to take care of this pig!" She had decided it was most definitely a pig, because what would an armadillo be doing in Ohio? When nobody answered, she added, "I'll carry it myself, I don't care!! I'M SAVING THAT PIG!"

She glanced at her brothers for support, but they were looking at her like they were pretty sure (but not *positive*) that she had lost her mind. Which she thought maybe was true. But! Dad wasn't looking at her like she was crazy. Dad was taking off his shirt. "Thank you, Daddy!" The shirt was his special blue one, with the logo from Jammer's team.

As Dad gently scooped up the pig in his shirt, his stomach protruding in that Dad way, Becca felt a wave of . . . of like she would *DESTROY* anyone who ever hurt her dad. She was almost shaking with emotion as she said again, "Thank you, Daddy."

Dad held the pig close. It was wrapped in the shirt, but still. Sarcoptic mange might be seeping through. And yet Dad embraced it like a human baby. It was not even a foot and a half long. Maybe it was only fifteen inches.

They walked quickly back to the house, Dad in front probably getting all mangy. Bailey motored his chair up to him, saying, "I want to see it closer, but it would be bad if I got mange. Really bad." But then he motored ahead and swung around. Dad paused while Bailey squinted at the pig. Then he moved to the side and said, "You better hurry, Dad!"

Becca jogged a couple of steps to catch up with her father. The pig had lifted its head a little, and it was clearly—*clearly*—pressing its head into Dad's belly. It did not seem scared at all. It seemed like it just loved being held by someone. It seemed like it thought it had gone to heaven. Becca was stunned at how *emotional* its tiny face was.

Dad was walking swiftly with long strides, his face filled with determination, like he was *absolutely* going to save this pig. She remembered she had asked him once how he felt the first time he held her, and he got a determined face and said,

"You were so tiny that you weren't out of danger yet. You still lived in intensive care. And I just thought, I am *not* going to let this child die."

That was what his face looked like now.

CHAPTER FIVE

SAUCY

If Dad gets mange, will he be mad at me? Becca wondered. But she thought he wouldn't. Because parents were like that, sometimes. Like that time Jammer lost his temper during a game and hit his $150 stick against the boards, and it cracked in the middle. Up in the stands, Dad leaned and held his face in his hands. He didn't look up until K.C. asked, "Yo, Dad, you crying?" He wasn't. But later he scolded Jammer, and Mom scolded Jammer, and Grandma *really* scolded him. And *then* Dad bought Jam another $150 stick. Because just about every hockey boy had done the same thing at least once.

Now, Dad occasionally broke into a brief jog.

"It likes being held," Dad called out during one of those jogs.

"How do you know, Jason?" Mom called back. "Maybe we shouldn't get too attached to this pig?" But then she added, "Poor little thing." As if maybe she was already getting a little attached herself.

"It's a leaner, like . . ." Dad trailed off. But Becca knew what he'd been about to say: like their cat, Shiner, who'd died. "And it's making noises, sighing."

Becca wanted to hear, so she edged closer, and, yes! She heard the pig sigh in a snorty, piggy way.

Without thinking, she reached toward it, but Dad said, "Stay back, Bec! Better safe than sorry, I always say."

It was true; he did always say that.

"Dad?" she asked. "Are we going to take my

pig to the animal hospital? Like, tonight?" She put the slightest emphasis on "my."

"Of course!" He said it so passionately that Becca could tell he was really liking this leaning, sighing, mangy pig.

At home, Mom made them wait outside with the piglet while she rushed in for garbage bags, plastic gloves, and a new shirt for Dad. As Dad put on the shirt, Mom lay the bags across the back seat of Dad's car. Then Dad gently lay the piglet down, tucking the blue shirt tightly around it and mumbling something about how much Becca used to love being wrapped in blankets. Becca put on gloves so that she could touch her pig. But her father was still mumbling! And then Mom started rearranging garbage bags! Becca heard a little whine coming out of her mouth. She hadn't meant to whine, but she did anyway. She wished they would hurry!

When they finally moved aside, she gently touched the pig's head. It felt exactly like she was petting a tree. She knew this for a fact, because once during a nature field trip, the guide had had the whole class pet a tree. It was thicker than Becca was tall, and probably hundreds of years old. And its bark felt like this piglet.

Then the piglet's eyelids fluttered, and it looked directly at her! And snorted! Not like it was sighing, but indignantly, like it was saying, *You know, it's about time you found me!*

"I'm going to call it Saucy!" Becca announced. "That means 'impertinent,' kind of like a smart aleck. When it's better, it's going to be impertinent. I can tell." Then tears filled her eyes, because what if the piglet couldn't get better? What if it really, really wanted to get better, but it couldn't? "Hurry! We have to get to the hospital!" She kind of shrieked that.

"Didn't one open on Barstow Boulevard?" Mom asked. "I remember driving by one time." Mom knew many things. She had to keep up with what was going on with all of them all the time, so her head was filled with information, including information she had never needed to use. Until she did.

Grandma leaned toward the car and surprised everyone by saying, "Poor Saucy! Mange can't be fun!"

Then Dad did a strange thing. He nudged Becca aside, saying, "Excuse me, Beccers," placed his gloved hands on Saucy's back, closed his eyes, and didn't speak for a full minute. Becca knew exactly what he was doing. Jammer's physical therapist healed patients like that. He had magic hands. Jammer needed a PT because his legs and back got super sore and stiff from all the hockey. And his PT, named Fuji, made it better, so he could keep playing. There were pictures of athletes all over Fuji's walls, with inscriptions like *To Magic Fuji, Thank you for healing me*. Fuji was half-Japanese, and if you were a famous athlete in the state, you had probably been to him.

Saucy was sighing again. "It's happy," Bailey

said, impressed. "You've got the magic pig hands, Dad."

Dad stood up, peeled off his gloves, and placed them in the garbage bag Mom was holding. Becca put hers in there too. Even though it was nearly bedtime, she got to go with Dad, since it was *her* pig and all. She sat in back watching Saucy the whole time, so it wouldn't fall off the seat.

Becca had seen Dad grab extra gloves, but she hadn't thought to bring any for herself. So if the pig actually did fall off, and she actually did pick it up, she would probably get sarcoptic mange and look like a tree for a while. But it would be worth it.

"Saucy?" she said. "Please don't die. Okay?" The pig didn't show that it heard her one way or another. So she said it again a little more loudly. "Saucy! Please don't die! Please? Okay?" She let her hand hover over the little pig, trying to send good thoughts through her hand the way Fuji might, and the way Dad just had. And again Saucy snorted indignantly! Like, *Do you even know what you're doing?*

And Becca knew she had picked the perfect name for her pig.

CHAPTER SIX

A *VERY* SICK PIG

At the animal hospital, the lady at the desk looked *so* surprised when she saw Saucy in Dad's arms. "My goodness!" she gasped. "My goodness!" She seemed genuinely disturbed. She was a really good person, Becca could tell.

"Follow me!" she ordered, and led them straightaway into an examination room without even asking their names or anything at all. A doctor burst in two minutes later. She looked very worried. "Hi, I'm Dr. Gibson. I hear you have a *very* sick pig!" She pulled on gloves and unwrapped Dad's shirt before examining Saucy briefly. "Ohhhhh. Ohh, my. That's the worst case of sarcoptic mange I've ever seen."

Jammer had been right!

Becca told Dr. Gibson how she had found the pig. She exaggerated a little bit, like she was kind of a hero. Although maybe she was? A hero? To the pig, anyway.

Dr. Gibson looked fascinated. "We're going to need to keep her here overnight. Would that be all right with you? Longer than just one night, actually. This is one sick pig."

"Yes, that's fine," Becca said quickly, then added, "She's a she?"

"Yes, she's a she. I'll call you personally first thing in the morning. We'll wash her with special shampoo, okay? And give her some medicine, and get her hydrated. We'll keep her as long as we have to, until you can take her home and begin shampooing her yourself."

"Yes, that's fine," Becca said quickly again.

She didn't look at Dad, because she knew that about right now he would be calculating how much this would all cost. She knew it would cost a lot, because their cat that was actually Bailey's had gotten hit by a car, and that cost $2,000, even with a "discount." And then he died anyway. That was Bailey's saddest life moment.

Dad said "Oh," as if surprised, and Dr. Gibson quickly added, "Since she's a rescue, we'll find a price we can both live with. How does that sound?"

Dad was an accountant, but they didn't have that much money, because of how expensive Jammer and Bailey were, and because Mom and Dad liked to save as much as they could in the bank. But finally Becca glanced at him. He was frowning. But it was a small frown. Barely a frown, actually.

"Dad, I'll—I'll be good my entire life and never argue with my brothers again, ever." She didn't know if that was possible, but she thought Dad might like it. Well, more accurately, she knew it was not possible at all, not even remotely. But Dad laid his hand on her shoulder, which, she had to admit, made her worry that mange might now be all over her shirt, because what if the mange had jumped onto him and his hand and now on her? But she decided to go for it, and she gave him a big hug. Because what was a little mange in the grand scheme of things?

CHAPTER SEVEN

GEEZ!

Lying in bed that night, Becca had a funny feeling that there was something she needed to remember. Or that she had to *do*. She thought it concerned Saucy. When she couldn't figure it out, she did something she knew was ridiculous: she held out her hand and kind of pointed it toward where the animal hospital was, three miles away. And she thought as hard as she could, *Get well, Saucy!*

The room kept lighting up. That would be Bailey taking selfies. He was a selfie addict. K.C. was reading in the dim light, even though this was probably bad for his eyes. She thought he secretly wanted glasses so that he would look super smart. Jammer was twisting his wrists in the air, just because he was always moving at least a little until he fell asleep.

Becca took a selfie as well. Most days she took three selfies a day. That was because there was a famous series of portraits of four sisters posing together every year for decades. The Brown sisters. And just seeing them change year after year was kind of amazing, or unsettling, or something. The pictures were in a local museum for a week once, and her whole family went. People looked at the pictures and actually cried. Over time passing, etc. Dad said so anyway. A strange feeling had washed over Becca as she viewed the pictures. In the beginning the sisters were young, and in the end they were old. Becca did not understand how this happened. She didn't understand at all.

Dad had stared at the Brown sisters and said, "Time waits for no one." He also said, "You can't

turn back time" and "How time flies!" It was weird how almost everything he said was kind of *boring*, but he wasn't boring himself, not a bit.

So anyway, since then, Becca had decided to take the three selfies a day. And then when she was very old, she would print out all the pictures, hang them up in the living room, and try to decide if she had done what she was supposed to do with her life.

Grandpa had made Becca and her brothers think about these things. Because he had written them a Serious Letter before he died. That's what it actually said across the top: *Serious Letter.* He said to figure out what you were supposed to do, because it would make you feel better than just about anything else would. Also, if you figured out that you were a bad person, you must figure out how to make yourself into a good person before you grew up. Because it was harder to do when you got old. He wrote them that letter because he'd loved them so much, even though none of them had so much as spoken a word yet. He'd died not long after they'd come home from the hospital. Dad said Grandpa had only stayed alive to make sure they got home okay. When he saw they were going to be fine, he died in his bed. From cancer. Sometimes when they went for walks, Becca looked up at the sky and wondered if he was still there watching them, or if he had moved on.

After Becca examined her new selfie, she put down her phone and closed her eyes, and she saw the pig, lying on the side of the road. Saucy must have known they were walking by, and that was why she had made noise. She was saying, *Help me!*

Becca opened her eyes. They had a projector night-light, so there was a Milky Way galaxy illuminating their ceiling. When they got the light last year was when K.C. suddenly had the idea they were living in a simulation. He said so right there in bed, and Becca had become scared. Because what if he was right?

Now, she closed her eyes, and again the vision of Saucy lying by the side of the road popped into her head. Suddenly her chest seemed to be experiencing actual, real, physical pain. She almost wondered whether she was having a heart attack. Was it even possible for an eleven-year-old to have a heart attack? She decided it was and clutched at her chest.

Because what if Saucy died in the night? What if she was dying right now? And now Becca's head was hurting too.

She jumped out of bed—she needed to call the animal hospital. Her brothers glanced over, then went right back into wherever their brains had been a moment earlier. Well, Bailey was still looking at her.

"Are you worried about the pig?" he asked, then added, "I can tell you are."

"It's just Becca," Jammer said. That was a little insulting, but she let it go because she had more important things on her mind.

She was already headed out to the hallway, pressing the numbers for the animal hospital.

"Tracks Animal Hospital! This is Teresa!" a woman answered enthusiastically, as if it were not a place full of sick animals, and as if it were not late at night.

Becca took a few steps down the hall. "Hi, I mean . . . hi! I brought my pig, Saucy, into the hospital tonight. I was wondering how she was doing."

"Is this Amanda?"

"Becca."

"Well, Becca, I watched them give Saucy a medicated bath just a little while ago. The doctor thinks she might make it."

"Might?"

"She's in pretty bad shape, Becca, darling. She's very, very weak. But she did show some life when we first began bathing her. She knows we're helping her. I've been working in animal care for seventeen years, and I know what the animals are thinking."

"Oh." Becca paused. "Does she miss me?"

"She surely does. She told me that as clearly as I'm telling you!"

Excitement rushed through Becca's whole body. Her face grew warm with it. "She misses me! Thank you. I'll come visit her tomorrow!"

"Okay, good night, sweet dreams."

"Good night!"

Becca stood in the hallway and felt love swell up in her heart. As hard as she could, she willed her pig to live. *Live. Live!* And she was sure the pig had somehow heard her, and had just snorted indignantly, like, *Of course I'll live! Geez!*

CHAPTER EIGHT

TRACKS ANIMAL HOSPITAL

Dad had to work the next day, and Mom was taking Bailey and Jammer to their physical therapists that morning, and the animal hospital said Becca couldn't visit Saucy until after ten a.m. So Becca nagged Mom and Dad *nonstop* about letting her go by herself if they couldn't take her, so that she could arrive at precisely ten. Finally, Mom and Dad decided it might be "good for Becca's confidence" to go to the hospital by herself and visit with the pig. Wait, did they think Becca didn't have enough confidence? Also, they said, "It would be good for you to make friends with this pig." What did that even mean? She didn't mind, though. She was excited to go alone! In case Saucy could eat, Becca was allowed to cut up Dad's avocado, the one he'd been waiting all week to get ripe. He loved avocado but made the big sacrifice for Saucy.

So there Becca was, bicycling down Barstow Boulevard, at nine forty a.m. She glanced at the baggie of avocado in her basket, feeling like she was about to meet the most important person in the world, if the most important person in the world had happened to be a pig.

At the hospital, the tech—a middle-aged woman with a lot of penguins on her scrubs—led her into a room lined with cages of sick animals. She smiled at Becca like Becca was seven years old or something. It was probably because she was wearing a new T-shirt that said I ♥ PIGS. Dad had gone out before he left for work to search for some kind of pig shirt that she could wear to the hospital. It made her feel a little guilty, though, because he'd had to throw away one of his favorite shirts after Saucy got it mangy.

And! Saucy already looked better! Little tufts of almost-hair stuck out here and there from her bark-like skin. Becca wanted to open the cage door and touch the pink, but she was scared to get mange. The tech gave her a raggedy towel, which Becca laid on the floor. Then she sat next to her pig's cage and just watched. Saucy was sleeping, taking deeper breaths than she had last night. Just by looking at her, Becca could tell she was doing much better.

The tech was cleaning out a cage a few feet away. "Excuse me?" Becca asked. "Do you know if my pig did well last night?"

The tech's eyes went bright. "Oh, I read her file. She did very well. We can all tell she has a fighting spirit."

"Thank you!" Becca said excitedly. She felt like . . . like she was "on cloud nine" and "had a new lease on life." She hadn't felt this excited since before everything bad had happened with MacKenzie.

So she just sat and watched Saucy and sang made-up songs about clouds and pigs and pig-shaped clouds. She felt sure Saucy liked that.

Saucy's ears were like little wings, like if the ears kept growing she would be able to fly someday. Pink skin peeked through the top edges. The pink gave Becca hope.

Less hopeful: an IV bag was dripping through a tube and into Saucy's front leg. Becca could vaguely remember from their cat that IVs cost a bunch of money. She couldn't remember how much. Would it be more than five hundred dollars? Because she knew that was how much Jammer's last skates cost. She felt like she had a lot of credit saved up, because she was for sure Mom and Dad's least expensive kid. Plus, she didn't know how much the totality of Jammer's hockey gear cost, but she was sure it was at least a thousand dollars. She knew this because every time he outgrew a piece of gear, her parents seemed disturbed. But then whenever they watched him play, it made them crazy happy.

"I'm all done here," the tech said. "Just stick your head out and give a shout if you need anything." She left the room.

Becca hesitated. She had an idea! She looked around the room until she found a box with gloves in it. She put on a pair, unlatched the cage door, and very, very gently laid her hands on Saucy, as if she were Fuji. Closing her eyes, she felt for a moment like she was hypnotizing herself. She tried to will the pig to understand that she was there—for *her*. She would not abandon

this pig for anything. Her eyes filled with tears—
she could feel Saucy's suffering! She could also
feel Saucy's love for her!

But when Becca opened her eyes, Saucy was
awake and looking *skeptically* at her. Like the pig
was thinking, *Wait a minute, you're not a real healer,
you're just a kid!*

Becca took a piece of avocado out—she would
bribe Saucy into loving her!—and held it in front
of Saucy's snout. The piglet opened her mouth,
suddenly happily expectant. So Becca placed the
avocado into her mouth. Saucy ate it like a con-
noisseur, like she was an avocado expert, even
though it was quite doubtful she'd ever eaten
an avocado before. Then she opened her mouth
again. Becca placed another piece of avocado in
there. This time Saucy didn't evaluate, just made
tiny, satisfied smacking noises.

As soon as she swallowed, Saucy opened

her mouth again, but now Becca was worried because she hadn't asked anybody if it was okay to feed Saucy. "I'll give you one more," she said. And she gave Saucy another, then put the bag to the side. But when Becca didn't give her still another, Saucy began to snort and snort. She impatiently waved her little hoof that had the IV in it! So Becca quickly gave her another, but then she was so worried that Saucy would pull the IV out that she got up, threw out her mangy gloves, and rushed out of the room.

In the waiting room, she told the receptionist what she had done. And the receptionist looked a little concerned! They both hurried into the sick-room, and . . . Saucy had closed her eyes and was resting peacefully.

Relief washed over Becca. "Next time I'll ask if I can feed her, I promise."

"Thank you," the receptionist said. She

seemed like she was trying to look stern, but she actually didn't look stern at all.

Suddenly Becca was *so* hungry. She'd left without eating breakfast. She said good-bye to Saucy. "So do you know when I can take my pig home?" she asked on the way out.

"I know the doctor was very pleased with how well she was doing this morning. But it all depends on how soon she gets truly well." She paused, then added firmly, "Which she will."

"Did the doctor say so?"

"The doctor did say so. She said she just had a feeling about this pig."

"Thank you. Um, I can—" Becca looked around. "I appreciate you taking such good care of my pig. I can sweep your floors or something to help out. I'm good at sweeping."

"That's *extremely* sweet of you. But it's not necessary. You just keep visiting. The animals heal faster when they have visitors. Okay?"

Becca didn't want to leave, not really, but she thought Saucy might have had enough activity for today. And since there was no sweeping to do . . .

"Well, bye."

"Bye, sweetie. Just keep being you!"

Becca hurried outside. It was hard to see because her eyes were getting teary. Partly because of how much she loved Saucy. But also because the receptionist had said, "Just keep being you!" She didn't know that Becca had bad parts inside of her.

She hopped onto her bike. It would be a fifteen-minute ride home. She'd been at the vet a whole two hours! That was weird. She tried to figure out how that could have happened. She didn't have any complicated theories about time like K.C. sometimes did; she just thought it was weird.

Between the heat and her helmet, sweat immediately began dripping down her face as she pedaled. Plus, she was so starving that it felt like something was chewing at her stomach. So halfway home, she stopped at a small shop for a snack. Everything cost more money than she had. She was so hungry! Mom said sometimes if people understood you, they would treat you differently. So Becca explained to the man at the counter about her pig, and he let her take some peanuts for all her change—just seventy-nine cents. As she was going out the door, he said, "Take care of that pig."

"Thank you, I will!"

So Mom was right.

Becca emptied the entire bag of peanuts into her mouth at once and chewed as she rode. Her sweat, her hunger, her visit with Saucy. It all felt very real to her. She didn't see how this could be some kind of a video game or simulation or whatever, like K.C. always said.

K.C. had watched *The Matrix* maybe more than a hundred times. While he didn't think it accurately depicted the simulation, it fascinated him anyway. It was one possible scenario for the simulation. The Bible in its way was another, K.C. said. He'd read something in the *New York Times* that said people had better not discover for sure if the world is a simulation, because if the "aliens" running the simulation realized that earthlings knew the truth, the aliens might decide to end it all . . . for some reason.

That would be bad. But Becca didn't believe it, even if it was in some big newspaper. Because no aliens would want to destroy a little pig. Why would they?

Every day Becca biked to the hospital. And every day Saucy was a little pinker, with more and more tufts of hair sticking out from the mange. When Becca arrived, Saucy always snorted *skeptically* at her, until she saw the baggie of avocado. Becca's mom had bought several when she heard how much Saucy liked them. Then her perfect little face would light up. It was unbelievable how perfect that pig was!

Saucy got better so fast that Becca only had to ride to the hospital five times, which from the look on Dad's face when he saw the bill, must have cost about a million dollars. All of them—

even Grandma— had piled into the family van to pick Saucy up. The good news was the vet said Saucy's recovery was a miracle and very, very unusual. When the vet said "very, very unusual," K.C. gave Becca a knowing look. "A sim glitch," he informed her. Well, maybe, K.C. Maybe.

As Dad paid the bill, he looked like he had that time Jammer broke his stick on purpose. Only worse. Guilt panged through Becca.

But Saucy! Saucy was now pink and fuzzy, with a couple of vaguely darker spots. Some tufts of hair were longer than the rest, giving her a disheveled look, but it was actually cute. She was already getting bigger—the receptionist said she was underweight at twenty pounds. "We think she's about nine weeks old, so she should actually weigh ten pounds more."

Becca held Saucy in her arms, rubbed nose against nose. She tried to remember another

time when her whole body had been as flooded
with love as it was now. But she couldn't remember such a time. Saucy felt like . . . like she was
denser than a cat or dog but not as dense as an
iron weight. She felt like a firm water balloon
except heavier than a water balloon would be.
Her hair was not even sort of soft. It was coarse
and crisp and *white*. The reason Saucy looked

pink was because that was the color of her skin. The areas around her eyes and nose were a little bit darker than everywhere else.

She felt warm in Becca's arms, like maybe she had a fever? Becca asked worriedly, "Is she supposed to feel so warm?"

"Pigs run a little warmer than humans," the receptionist explained. "Even 104 degrees would be within the normal range."

"Okay, then everything is fine?"

"Everything is fine. But before you leave, Dr. Gibson wants to talk about some things."

That didn't sound good. It was never good when a doctor wanted to talk to you about "some things." Or a dentist. Every time their dentist needed to talk to them after a check-up, it was bad news. Becca nodded, but she felt like she might be having her second heart attack. At age eleven and a half.

In a minute, Dr. Gibson came out and said, "Sooo . . ." They all waited. "So it's important to know that this is a Yorkshire. Yorkshires are farm pigs. And farm pigs get very big. Six or nine months from now she may weigh three hundred pounds, if fed properly. If you kept her, she could eventually weigh more than six hundred."

Becca tilted her head, as if that would help her understand better. Nobody spoke until Dad said, "The silence is deafening." Becca couldn't think of even one thing to say. She herself weighed *eighty-seven* pounds. She said it out loud. "Oh, wow. I mean, I weigh eighty-seven."

"Then Saucy is going to weigh about six point nine times more than you," K.C. said. "I just did that in my head. Of course, you'll gain some weight over the next year as well, so . . ."

Sometimes it was hard to follow what K.C.'s

specific point was. The pig was going to be *big*, that was the only point that mattered.

Becca turned to her father. "But Dad!" she cried out. She turned to her mother. "But Mom! *Mom!* Don't you want a pet pig?"

"Honey," said Mom. "A lot of our backyard is concrete. It's not even that big. . . ."

"Can we move to a farm?" Becca breathed in Saucy's sweet, musty smell. She knew the answer would be no. She knew that. She closed her eyes, tried to think.

"There's a pig sanctuary that I know of," the vet said gently. "They really love their pigs. I've been there. The pigs there are very happy."

Becca nodded without looking up, still smelling that sweet, musty smell.

"Well," Dad said. Becca looked hopefully at him. He put his hand on his heart. "This all truly tugs at my heartstrings."

Becca's heart rose; then fell: six hundred pounds was about what her entire family except for Dad weighed *altogether*. And an animal that big might hurt Bailey. And another thing, where would it live exactly? Then she asked the vet, "How much would a six-hundred-pound pig eat a day?"

"Maybe ten pounds of food?" the doctor replied. "To be honest, I don't work with many farm animals. And usually—I'm being honest here—most pigs that big, they would be, uh . . ."

"Eaten," Jammer said.

Becca shot a worried glance at Saucy, but of course she didn't understand a word of human talk. In fact, she was smiling up at Becca. For certain, it was a smile, her pretty little mouth curved up at the ends. She was already feeling heavy in Becca's arms, but Becca didn't set her down. In fact, she held her tighter.

"I would say . . . I would say, to give her a chance to fully recover, we could keep her until she weighs a hundred," Mom said, then added quickly, "Or maybe fifty or sixty."

Becca was starting to feel sick. "But how long will it take for her to reach a hundred pounds?" she asked in a wobbly voice.

"Maybe fifty or sixty," Mom repeated.

"It depends on the pig, although the way they're bred, it's fairly predictable. Figure, maybe three months is what we're talking about." Dr. Gibson was a thin woman with worried eyes. Becca had seen her quite a few times in the last few days, and she always looked worried about the animals. But now she looked *very* worried.

Becca took a big breath, then decided to put it out of her head that she might . . . probably . . . actually *would* have only a short time with Saucy.

She decided to focus on *now*. She raised her own eyes to Mom, the Great Scheduler. "Do we have time to go get pig food?"

The vet had written down exactly what they should buy: either ready-made feed or beans (which needed to be cooked), grains, and various vegetables. Lettuces, spinach, dandelion, kale, endive. Turnips. Cucumber. Yam. Even an egg once in a while. And fruit. Mom went inside a farm supply store to buy feed. But they all went into the grocery store together to pick out the vegetables, because Becca wanted to choose them personally. And her brothers wanted to be wherever the new pig was. At first the Great Scheduler had pointed out that Becca always took a long time to pick out anything at all, like the time she spent three hours picking out the flower seeds for her garden that she hadn't taken care of.

Becca in turn pointed out that it was *her* pig, and she had to make sure that the doctor's list was followed *exactly*. And then the boys backed her up, and all four of them said they absolutely had to bring the pig into the store as the car would get too hot, and then Saucy might need to go to the hospital again from heat something . . . they weren't sure what it was called when you got too hot. But for sure it was bad! When all of them banded together over something, their parents usually said yes, unless it was something that was hurtful in some way. So after a torrent of begging, Mom and Dad gave in. Mom and Dad were not very good at facing a torrent.

"You spoil your kids! I didn't spoil my kids," Grandma scolded. "Nope, didn't happen."

As Becca carried Saucy into the store, other customers looked surprised, but in a good, smiling way. Becca felt quite proud!

But when they got to the produce section, the little pig went berserk! She began barking almost like a dog! Whining. Squealing. She squealed so loud Becca was sure every single person in the store could hear. And then she managed to squirm free, falling to the floor with a thump and a grunt. She started running back and forth, as if she couldn't decide what to do first. There was

so much she *could* do! There was a lettuce leaf that had fallen to the ground. She grabbed that, and it was gone in an instant. Becca scrambled to pick Saucy up, but the piglet was off again! She jumped up to nip at a banana, and suddenly she was running off with a banana in her mouth. When someone shouted, she dropped the banana and barked at two random people, neither of whom were the one who had shouted. She bolted away squealing. Becca and her family chased after her, screaming, "Saucy! Saucy!"

Saucy raced past the canned foods, found the cereal aisle, and just as Becca slid around the corner, Saucy *assaulted* a box of oatmeal! She'd already ripped it open—oatmeal flakes flying through the air—by the time Becca was able to grab her up. She held Saucy extra tight, and Saucy promptly peed all over Becca's I ♥ PIGS T-shirt!

"I'll take her back to the van!" Becca cried,

running out of the store. Unfortunately, she didn't have the keys. But Saucy, away from the food, had suddenly calmed down, and then Dad came up from behind and opened the van door.

Becca got in with her now extremely peaceful pig. Bailey had followed Dad and motored up his ramp. "That pig is crazy," he said, his voice full of admiration.

Dad said Mom was still inside with Grandma, Jammer, and K.C. buying the vegetables, paying for the ripped-open box of oatmeal, and apologizing to whomever needed apologizing to. Then he got behind the wheel and started the car, leaving the motor running, as if they might need to make a quick getaway. Meanwhile, Saucy sniffed at the pee on Becca's shirt and looked up at her with bright, very, very innocent eyes.

"I know, you didn't mean to cause trouble," Becca told her. "I love you so much!" She thought a moment, then added, "Not to worry, Mom will clean my shirt." Although Saucy didn't look worried at all!

When the others returned, Becca noted that they had only two bags of groceries. How long would that last? "Is that enough food?" she asked worriedly.

"We can always come back when we need to," Mom said.

Saucy was going berserk again. Becca held her as tightly as she possibly could. "Buckle up!" Dad shouted, screeching out of the parking lot. Dad was usually such a safe driver!

Saucy squealed like she was in torment. "Oh, I'm sorry!" Becca cooed, and loosened her grip, just a tiny bit. But that little bit was all Saucy needed to wriggle hard and *hurl* herself to the floor. She ran snorting to the groceries. "I think she's hungry!" Becca cried out.

"DUH!" Jammer said. But he turned around to watch Saucy disappear into a grocery bag. The bag started wiggling and shaking.

"What's happening back there?" Dad asked nervously.

"Just drive, hon," Mom replied.

Thank goodness they lived barely a mile from the grocery store. As soon as Dad was pulling into the driveway, Becca unbuckled her seat belt and pulled Saucy out of what was now a destroyed cloth bag. All that was left in that bag were two leaves of kale and a few unattached celery stalks. Also half a zucchini. Somehow, a shred of kale was stuck up one of Saucy's nostrils.

"There's a hole in the bottom of the bag," K.C. said, as if she couldn't see for herself. He was squinting, even though the bag was right there in front of him.

Becca's heart nearly exploded with pride.

"Saucy, what a good eater you are!"

But Saucy now seemed so exhausted that she went limp as Becca carried her into the backyard. Becca's zafu was out there, right where she'd left it. Saucy climbed on it and fell asleep. Becca hissed, "Nobody bother her!" She ran inside to wash her stomach and change into her T-shirt that said, DON'T GROW UP. IT'S A TRAP! Grandma gave each of them one "funny" T-shirt every Christmas. Then whenever you wore one of her T-shirts, she would chuckle as she read whatever it said.

Anyway, back outside, Saucy was making soft snoring noises and twitching her nose and lips like she was dreaming. At first the entire family all gathered around and watched her. Then Mom, Dad, and Grandma got hot and went inside. Every time one of Becca's brothers made any noise at all, she shot them a look. Saucy slept and slept.

Waiting for Saucy to wake up, Becca decided

to try to meditate. She folded her legs on the concrete and closed her eyes, but her mind kept drifting to Saucy, and then her heart would start racing with joy. Finally she opened her eyes again and just watched her pig.

K.C. read on his phone, his leg leaning against the zafu right where one of Saucy's legs was hanging off. Bailey hummed and wrote lyrics on his phone, but the sound was soft enough that Becca allowed it. Jammer did some push-ups and stretching, but then got up abruptly to hit pucks into his net. He did that all the time, where it suddenly just occurred to him that he *needed* to be hitting pucks. The noise of the *whack* made Saucy squeal. Her eyes opened wide with terror. "STOP IT! STOP IT RIGHT NOW!" Becca shouted. But the yelling surprised Saucy even more, and she started *crying*. And snorting.

And then she bit into the zafu and ran off with

it. Then she dropped it and ran toward Jammer with her head bowed. She tried to ram into him, right into his calf. As a joke, Jammer started running and saying, "Help me!" Saucy raced after him, and as soon as he stopped, she bowed her little head again like she wanted to ram him. But instead she just stared at him for a moment, and raised her nose into the air like she didn't *even* have time to ram anyone. So he walked by her, and she rammed him after all—it was a sneak attack! Jammer smiled, and Saucy smiled back. Friends.

"I told you that pig was crazy," Bailey said admiringly. "That's the dopest pig I ever met!"

CHAPTER TEN
PIG-AMONIUM

So then: A pig is *NOT* a dog. Not that Becca had ever owned a dog, but she'd had friends with dogs. The first night home with Saucy, Dad put up an old baby gate in the kitchen and set up a dog bed he'd bought at the big discount pet supply store in the next town over. The bed had a lime-green psychedelic print. That was on account of Dad had gone to the store with Bailey, and Bailey picked out the print because it was crazy like the pig.

And Becca had to admit that Saucy looked quite cute on lime green. Saucy also dragged the zafu to the bed, where she suddenly ripped into it with great satisfaction. But there were issues:

Why couldn't Saucy sleep in bed with Becca? Because, Grandma declared, that would only happen over her dead body! "No pigs in the bedrooms!"

Then *why* couldn't Becca sleep in the kitchen with Saucy? Because, Mom said, no child of hers would be sleeping on the kitchen floor for weeks.

Well, *why* couldn't Saucy sleep with Becca in the living room? Because, Dad said, there was carpeting in the living room, and Saucy might pee or poop.

So even though Becca had, yes, tried to manipulate her parents into changing their minds by frowning and sticking out her lower lip like she might cry, they didn't change their minds. But the thing was, Becca felt really sad inside, because as Becca backed out of the kitchen, Saucy looked at her like, *Why are you leaving me?* In fact, Becca felt as terrible inside as she did that time Grandma was in the hospital for three days. Even though Grandma drove her crazy.

So Saucy ended up in the kitchen alone for her first night. Becca and her brothers lingered at the gate while Saucy stared forlornly at them from the other side. Then, all of them terrifically sad, they went to their bedroom and got in bed. And were asleep in an instant. Because something about getting a new pig was *extremely* tiring.

Becca and her brothers slept quietly. Saucy was silent. Mom was asleep with no children sleeping on the kitchen floor. Grandma was asleep with no pigs sleeping with her grandchildren in the bedroom. Dad was asleep, satisfied that he'd found Saucy an excellent, though psychedelic, bed. The night was quiet, all right.

Then, early in the morning, just as the sky was turning gray, there was a mind-boggling commotion, as if ten full-grown pigs were ripping apart the kitchen cabinets.

Becca leaped out of bed so quickly she lost her balance and fell facedown. She pushed herself up and ran toward the commotion, crying out, "I'm coming, Saucy!" As she rounded the corner toward the kitchen, she saw Saucy's face light up as if she hadn't seen Becca in a year. Becca paused, soaking in the pleasure at seeing her pig again, but then Saucy furiously rammed into the guard gate, and bashed it right over! She clambered past the fallen gate and ran headlong into Becca's legs.

Becca scooped Saucy up. "I missed you, too!" She swayed back and forth, Saucy snorting happily. Saucy had the cutest eyelashes! But! Bailey was talking from the kitchen floor where he'd pulled himself—he did not usually like to use a wheelchair inside the house. "Wow, Saucy, WOW," he was saying.

K.C. also added, "WOW, Becca, WOW."

Jammer said, "Holy *frick.*"

Becca stepped over the kitchen threshold. And, well, WOW. It did actually look like ten pigs had ripped apart the kitchen cabinets. Three cabinet doors had been ripped off their hinges!

And somehow, there were three drawers on the floor. How did Saucy even reach them? Two chairs lay on their sides, one with a broken leg. And, of course, the covered trash can lay on its side, uncovered, and Becca was pretty sure some of what had been in there was now in Saucy's bulging belly.

Mom, Dad, and Grandma stood in in the middle of the mess, Dad looking strangely calm, nodding as if this were all part of some grand plan.

For a second there, Becca was torn between a respectful awe that Saucy was capable of such destruction, and being . . . *horrified.* In her mind, she pictured the workmen installing those cabinets just last summer. She remembered Grandma saying with satisfaction, "These are quality cabinets. They'll last forever."

Bailey was gaping as he looked all around. He turned to Becca and said, "Wow." Then his face lit up. "That pig is nuts. I like her!"

Mom's mouth was moving, but at first, no words came out.

Then, even though a couple of cabinets were *destroyed*, she uttered weakly, "Huh, she ate part of your zafu."

Becca cleared her throat and announced loudly, "It wasn't her fault! She's new, she doesn't know house rules yet. Pleeeeease don't blame Saucy!"

Grandma snapped, "I don't like crazy pigs!"

"Mom, I'm going to start cleaning up right now!" Becca practically screamed. She put Saucy down, rushed to the cabinet under the sink, and pulled out some kind of sprayer-soap stuff. "I'm doing it *right now*, Mom!"

And . . . cleaning up ended up being fun, with Saucy following her around from here to there, and from there to here, back and forth across the kitchen. Becca liked having a pig follow her every step. She liked it a lot.

K.C. and Bailey helped fix the cabinets, leaning against each other as they looked up directions on the Internet, just because they were multiples and leaned on each other sometimes. They learned the difference between a Phillips and a slotted screwdriver. Saucy watched quite closely, as if she too were learning how to fix cabinets. Jammer took off with Mom because he had a skate, and at one point Grandma sat in the kitchen, bossing around the rest of them. When Bailey stopped for lemonade, Grandma snapped,

"Do something useful, young man!" She also scolded Saucy, "YOU are a bad pig."

"She's not a bad pig, Grandma, she's a crazy pig. There's a big difference," Bailey explained.

"I know my pigs," Grandma retorted. Whatever that meant. Like, which pigs did she know?

Still, they all said, "Yes, Grandma, you know your pigs." But then Grandma, perhaps tired from so much bossing and scolding, went to take a nap.

Cleaning up took hours if you included vegetable and bathroom breaks, as well as breaks when it turned out that Saucy didn't actually have to use the bathroom but Becca hadn't been sure. Becca decided not to give Saucy feed that day—who knew how much garbage she'd eaten? She wasn't sure if that was the right thing to do—Saucy needed her nutrients—but it was, as Dad liked to say, "an executive decision."

Dad came home at lunch with something new for Saucy. He had read up on pigs during a coffee break and found directions on how to train your pig to use a harness and leash. Then he'd spent half his lunch break buying stuff for Saucy so they could take her on walks.

He left the directions on the kitchen table before returning to work. Becca read them through—it didn't look hard. She thought her brothers would help, but they went off to play video games. That was fine—she'd be alone with her pig for the first time since they'd come home!

Saucy loved the backyard. She sniffed around like a detective figuring out a crime. She didn't pay any attention at all to Becca while she sniffed, so Becca looked up videos of people walking their pigs. And found some! Then, as happens when you're on YouTube, she got distracted by other videos, including pigs eating, pigs running, pigs

101

jumping, and even pigs being born. When she finally looked up, Mom's vegetable garden was . . . well, it was gone. And the guilty party had dirt all over her face. And was looking extremely satisfied.

Panic made Becca feel like she needed more air. Mom loved her garden! A lot. She took a deep breath and quickly tried to replant some of the plants, but she couldn't get them to stand up anymore; how had they wilted so fast? She tried to figure out what to do. She remembered Jammer's standard backup plan any time he'd broken a window with a puck. *I'll make it up to Mom and Dad!* She propped the stalks up with mounds of dirt, then cleaned off Saucy's face. She would make this up to Mom!

Then she put the harness on Saucy, which admittedly was quite a struggle. It was kind of epic, to be honest. Saucy clearly did not understand what Becca was doing, or why. She got a suspicious look in her eyes and ran to the far side of the yard. But Becca had never been so determined in her life. She wanted to be able to show off her pig on her family's nightly walks. She cornered Saucy, crouched down, and grabbed her firmly. At one point, she was actually *wrestling* with her pig. It was hard to believe how strong and wiggly and squirmy a little pig was. But Becca won! Once the harness was on, Saucy completely calmed down, as if the previous ten minutes hadn't even happened. Following the directions, Becca attached one end of the leash to one of the very sturdy poles holding up the laundry line and hooked the other end onto Saucy, who didn't even seem to notice. Then Becca went inside to get some baby carrots.

When she came out, Saucy was back to her detective work, sniffing intently at the ground.

Becca set down a few carrots close to the pole. Saucy snorted with happy surprise and gobbled them up. She then looked expectantly at Becca, who took a few steps back, holding out another carrot. Saucy moved eagerly toward her. The leash pulled taut, and Saucy's eyes widened in panic. She squealed and screamed and tried to run free, panicking more every time the leash tightened. Her screaming started to sound human!

Becca started screaming as well, trying to grab Saucy so she could free her. They began wrestling again. Finally Jammer, who must have just gotten home, ran up yelling, "Whoa, whoa, whoa!" He snatched Saucy up and unhooked her. Saucy leaned her head into his chest and gave Becca an accusing glare. It was true: it was accusing, and it was a glare.

"I'm sorry, Saucy, I'm sorry. I just wanted to take you for a walk with us at night! Don't you want to go for a walk with us?" She tried to pet Saucy, but Saucy turned her head away. Big-time snub.

Then something seemed to occur to Saucy, and she began to squirm. Jammer set her down, and she dashed off to eat some carrots that Becca must have lost while they were wrestling.

Becca still had a few carrots in her pocket, and Saucy ate them right from her hand while occasionally stopping to smile at her. The wrestling matches, the leash pulling taut—all forgotten!

CHAPTER ELEVEN

BATHTIME

Saucy was, however, *very* dirty. In fact, her hooves and snout were brown from digging in Mom's garden. The garden that didn't exist anymore. The vet had given Becca special medicated shampoo and had told her to wash Saucy daily for two more weeks. And as Dad would say, "There's no time like the present." Which was usually not true . . . But never mind!

The vet's exact words: *Just put her in the tub with lukewarm water, even if she resists.* She'd said it was important, to make sure the mange would not return.

Saucy happily followed Becca inside and

into the bathroom. She seemed to love to follow Becca. Saucy twirled happily as the water ran.

But when the tub had filled, Becca hesitated. What did the vet mean about Saucy resisting? Becca took a big breath, whistled it out, then lifted Saucy into the tub—where she immediately let loose with an ear-exploding squeal, like she was being *killed*. Becca froze, quickly tested the water: it was lukewarm. She said in her sternest voice (which probably wasn't all that stern), "The vet says this is important!" So as long as Saucy was already in the water, Becca decided to quickly shampoo her, because owning a pig obviously involved all kinds of quick executive decisions. The squealing made Becca feel as if she really were killing the little pig! But she had to do it, she had to!

Grandma, K.C., and Bailey had crowded into the bathroom, yelling, "What's wrong?"

Then Mom and Jammer ran in just as Becca was shouting, "I'M GIVING HER A BATH!"

"You're killing her!" Bailey shouted. "Mom, she's killing the pig!"

Saucy's squealing morphed into something almost otherworldly, as if this were the actual most painful experience in the history of the world. She kicked and splashed until Becca could hardly see through all the water in her eyes. The whole ordeal, including rinsing, took maybe three minutes. Then Becca lifted Saucy out, and they both lay on the bathroom floor on their backs, recovering from their trauma. Saucy's little hooves stuck straight up into the air.

Becca didn't know how long they lay there. But then she heard K.C. calling, "Bec! The police are here! They want to see the pig!"

She sat up. *What?* Saucy hopped to her feet. Becca picked her up and walked uncertainly to

the living room. Where two police officers were standing just inside the doorway. A neighbor hovered behind them.

One of the officers asked, "This is the pig that was making all that noise?"

"She didn't like her bath," Becca explained.

The other officer laughed. The neighbor said, "It sounded like somebody was getting killed. I never heard a voice so loud in my life."

"I'm very sorry, officers," Mom said, holding out her hand to shake. "It won't happen again." She paused as the officers shook her hand, then continued, "That is, it may not happen again. I don't think it will happen again, in any event."

So the police left, with Grandma calling after them, "Why don't you take the pig with you?"

CHAPTER TWELVE

THE LIST

And yet every day after that, Saucy seemed to enjoy her bath immensely. Becca wondered if Saucy had only been trolling her the first time, just like Grandma might. But there were more issues.

Every evening, Becca made notes on things she had to make up to her parents. After three days and nights, there were thirty-seven items on the list, some more important than others. Like the night Saucy nosed open the refrigerator and the freezer too, and all the frozen food melted. And all the vegetables got eaten. And the bottom refrigerator drawer got broken. And

Mom said tiredly, "I'll have to get online and see if we can replace that." Becca did not like to see Mom speak tiredly, because in general Mom was a high-energy person. When Mom was tired, it made them all feel guilty. Like the time Jammer wanted to skate six days a week, and they tried that for two months. And Mom got so tired that she cried, because she really, really wanted to be able to take Jammer to the rink six times a week. But she couldn't, because some of the skates were at five in the morning and lasted for several hours. Altogether, it was a lot of time for Mom to be sitting in the freezing rink doing nothing except scheduling in her head.

Sometimes when Saucy did something naughty, Becca tried to fix it. So like, with the refrigerator, she attempted gluing the drawer together and sliding it back in place. It looked convincing, but it fell apart the first time Mom tried pulling it out. And that too made Mom seem tired.

Becca and K.C. spent hours putting child locks on all the cabinets. Plus, every night they put the garbage can and chairs on top of the table so that Saucy couldn't get at them. All of that worked pretty well. One child lock did get broken, but only one. Still, Becca added that child lock to her list. She planned to be honest and transparent!

On the optimistic side, every day Saucy got very slightly better with the leash.

One morning everybody except Becca and Grandma went to the rink with Jammer. Saucy had dragged her bed from the kitchen to the bathroom, which was what she did whenever Becca was about to take a shower. Sometimes she also dragged what was left of the zafu.

This time, when Becca got out of the shower, Saucy was sitting right there, like always. Except . . .

except . . . she had that *look* on her face. Like she was proud of some really excellent thing she had done. Becca saw that there were strips of cloth on the psychedelic bed. Saucy looked up at her, her eyes beaming. The strips of cloth looked like . . . the living room curtains. For just the briefest moment, Becca thought she knew precisely how Mom felt when she got that tired look.

"Saucy" was all she could say. Then she gathered energy and said forcefully, "Saucy!"

Saucy grabbed her bed in her mouth and ran off with it to the kitchen. Becca was right behind her. The little pig let go of her bed in the middle of the kitchen, jumped on it, and looked at Becca like a queen, like *I know you can't scold me when I'm sitting on my bed*. Becca actually knew this feeling. Her parents always said that she and her brothers were safe in bed, regardless of what had happened during the day, regardless of whether anyone had argued together or been scolded or in any way gotten in any trouble at all. In bed, you slept safely, and when you got up, it was a new day. So it wasn't really possible to scold Saucy now, was it? She tried to think what Mom and Dad might do. And she remembered that every time one of them had gotten scolded, once they were in bed, her parents made a point of saying "I love you" to the one who'd been scolded. Whenever this had happened to Becca, she tried to be extra good the next day.

So she decided to say it to Saucy: "I love you, Saucy." Because Saucy was on her bed.

Next Becca went to examine the damage.

It was bad.

Both curtain panels lay on the floor, along with the curtain rod. One panel was in shreds. Admittedly, Becca's first thought was, *How can I hide this?* Which wasn't very honest and transparent. So she took out her phone and added *living room drapes* to the list of things she had to make up for.

She carefully folded up the curtains. The good thing was that she was pretty sure they weren't expensive. In general, Mom and Dad were not into super-nice things around the house. Jammer got the best skates and gear, and Bailey got the best wheelchair and physical therapist, and their van had been new when they bought it. Otherwise, Becca did not think anything else in their lives was the best you could get. Relief flowed through her, because no matter what Saucy destroyed, it was usually kind of okay. Right? That was what Becca told herself anyway.

She lifted Saucy onto the couch with her, and together they watched a cartoon about pigs that Becca found on a cartoon channel. Saucy was surprisingly interested. She climbed down,

walked right up to the TV, and stood in front of it, staring. When Grandma came in, she didn't even notice the curtains. She said, "Sunny day. Huh!" As if sunny days were just an annoyance she had to deal with sometimes. Then she headed for the kitchen, probably for her midmorning snack.

When the others came home, Becca ran straight up to Mom to explain. But before she could say anything, Saucy ran up to Mom and Dad and began wagging her curly tail and spinning, like she was *very* excited to see them.

Both of them said, "Awwwww" and knelt down and petted her. Mom said, "You know, sometimes I look at her face and just think it's one of the cutest things I ever saw." Those words made Becca's heart sing.

"She certainly is cute," Dad agreed. Then he said, "Wait, where are the curtains?"

Gah! "I'm going to make it up to you!" Becca

cried out. She threw her arms around Saucy. "She didn't mean it! I read that pigs like to nest!" Her parents were staring at the big curtainless window. "I'll bet the curtains cost a lot less than Jammer's skates!" Becca blurted out, shooting a mean look at Jammer.

"Whoa!" Jammer exclaimed, as if she'd just slapped him, even though by now she'd probably said that five times since they got Saucy.

"I like the extra sunlight," Bailey mused. "I like the pig, too." He pulled himself onto the couch with a grunt and gazed at the bare windows. "Nice window—it looks bigger now," he added.

Grandma was walking through, no doubt having finished her snack. "Sunny day. Huh!" she said again, then continued to her room.

K.C. looked from the window to Saucy. "This is one weird simulation. It's kinda crazy to think

some alien somewhere thought all this up a billion years ago."

But as usual, nobody knew what he was talking about.

And Mom was no longer looking at Saucy like she was one of the cutest things that she had ever seen. She looked tired. Not quite as tired as she'd been when she'd tried to drive Jammer to the rink six times a week, plus take care of all Bailey's medical needs, plus buy groceries, plus clean the house, and so on. But she was tired; clearly, she was.

CHAPTER THIRTEEN

THE KITCHEN FLOOR

Mom was a light sleeper, and she said that every night she could hear Saucy whining in the middle of the night. So she announced to Becca with defeat in her voice, "I guess I'm going to have to let you sleep on the kitchen floor with a pig." But then she smiled and added, "Someone advised me when you were all babies to just let you cry, but I could never do it. I can't even stand listening to a pig cry. So just enjoy sleeping with her while we still . . ."

Becca's eyes went wide. "You mean while we still have her?" she asked in a small voice.

Mom touched Becca's cheek with her palm.

"You're a good girl. She's a good pig. She is. Just have fun with her, okay?"

Becca had to make an executive decision: Should she pout, or should she celebrate that she could sleep with Saucy? She decided to celebrate by eating carrots with her pig. First she ate one while Saucy waited patiently, and then Saucy ate one. They took turns until there were no more left, and Becca felt like she never wanted to see a carrot again—she had never even liked carrots!

That night, Saucy's face looked just like a startled child's when she realized that Becca would be staying with her in the kitchen. She celebrated by running around the table snorting, then stopping to twirl around, then whining and panting. Then she stood on her bed and wagged her tail with her mouth open extra wide in what was most definitely a big smile.

Becca and her brothers each owned a small

rechargeable lamp that they kept by their beds in case of an emergency that had never occurred. Becca brought hers with her to the kitchen, as well as her phone and charger, and a cup of water. All her nighttime items. She felt very at home on the kitchen floor in her flowered sleeping bag and fell right to sleep.

She woke up the first time with Saucy lying on top of her legs. "Saucy, you have to move," she said sleepily. Saucy didn't wake up, so with a bit of a struggle, Becca moved her legs. Since Saucy was on the bottom of the sleeping bag, Becca had to lie with her legs out from under the covers. But it was summer, and the air felt good on her legs!

When she woke up next, Saucy had moved up, her head now lying on Becca's stomach. That felt kind of comforting, but at the same time, the pressure on Becca's ribs made it hard to sleep. So she just lay on the hard floor, leaving the sleeping bag for Saucy. Which was fine—perfectly comfortable! She felt happy!

She woke up in the morning to find her brothers surrounding her with their phones out, taking pictures.

"Your lamp's broke," Jammer said, snapping a picture.

The plastic shade had broken off the main part of the lamp. And the water was spilled. But, thankfully, not on the phone. The charger cable was chewed through, however.

"Cables don't cost much," Becca said immediately. Still, she sat up and added *phone cable* to her list of things she had to make up for. She examined the lamp, saw it wasn't fixable, and added that as well. Then she and her brothers sat on the floor with Saucy, and they all ate their breakfasts together. When Saucy ran out of pellet feed and

cucumbers, she flipped a kitchen chair over with her nose. Becca sprang up and checked the chair for damage, but it was fine. She decided to try having a serious talk with her pig. "Saucy, you can't just flip a chair over when you don't get your way."

Saucy seemed to know exactly what Becca was saying—and she didn't like it. In fact, she *squinted* at Becca. Then she said, "Hmmmm." Like she was *judging* Becca.

Jammer laughed. "Oh, you got a lot of authority with that pig, don't you?" he said. Saucy's face lit up, like Jammer was quite amusing . . . or else Becca was imagining all this. Could this pig be that smart?

Then, reading her mind, Bailey said, "That's one smart pig!"

That made Becca feel quite proud, as if she were somehow responsible for Saucy's intelligence. So what if she was a little destructive?

"Come, Saucy!" she said happily. She walked to the bathroom to take her shower, Saucy dragging her dog bed as she followed. As Becca got into the shower, she could hear Bailey singing from the other side of the door, and when she got out of the bathroom, all three of her brothers were on the floor around the pig's bed. Bailey was singing while Jammer and K.C. petted Saucy. Saucy's eyes were closed, her nose slightly raised, as if she smelled something very, very good. How quickly she had gone from almost dying of mange to Most Spoiled Pig!

At lunchtime Dad came home all excited. "Look what I found!" he exclaimed. Becca didn't have the slightest idea what it was. Some kind of huge book. "A phone book!" Dad continued. "Watch this! I read that some pigs like this because of their nesting instinct."

He set it on the kitchen floor, and Saucy pushed at it with her nose. After a few pushes, she grabbed at it and ripped a piece off. This seemed to please her a lot, and she lay down and ripped and ripped. Ripped for so long the boys got bored and went to play Xbox. And Dad was long gone.

Becca stayed with Saucy. What didn't make sense was that she felt completely at peace, even though all she was doing was sitting on the kitchen floor, watching a little pig shred paper. She was sure this was much more relaxing than meditating. As a matter of fact, she thought everybody should just throw away their zafus and watch a pig tear up a phone book instead.

CHAPTER FOURTEEN

SAUCY GOES FOR A WALK

It took nearly a week for Saucy to get completely used to the leash and harness. Five days in a row she panicked, but less each day, and on the sixth day she suddenly *got* it. She had gained six pounds in that time. Becca weighed Saucy every morning by first weighing herself, then picking up Saucy and stepping on the scale again. Currently Saucy was twenty-six pounds, so it would be a lonnnng time before Becca had to give her up. Right? On the other hand, it was a little disturbing how much Saucy ate, and how quickly she was growing. So Becca decided to simply stop weighing her: she did not want to know the truth.

They took Saucy for her first walk that very night. The sky was clear, and a couple of stars were already shimmering, which was just the way Becca felt walking her pig, like she was shimmering.

"Why do we have to be the family with the pig?" Grandma grumped. "Why can't we just be a normal family?"

"Sometimes it's good to go off the beaten path," Dad said thoughtfully. "March to a different drummer. You don't want to live your life in the middle of the road."

"I do," Grandma replied. "That's exactly where I want to live. Now people will think we're crazy."

"The pig's crazy, Grandma," Bailey said. "We're not."

Actually, Becca was barely paying attention to the conversation, because Saucy was pulling so very hard that they were rushing along in front of everybody else. Then, right as they were passing the place where they had found Saucy, the pig stopped short and squealed, as if she'd walked into an invisible wall.

Becca felt it too, a wall of warmth against her face and whole body. It wasn't hot, like when you opened the oven door. It was almost not there. Except it was. She stood still to try to figure out where it was coming from. But when she looked around, all was tranquil: the trees under the half-moon in the gray sky, the patch of wild daisies a few feet away, the peaceful, empty road. It was a perfect night! Still, she could feel that change in the air . . . right . . . here.

She walked through it—it lasted a few feet. "Did anybody else feel that?" she asked.

"Now what?" Grandma asked irritably.

"Feel what, sweetheart?" Mom asked, already past the wall.

They'd all gone right through the wall. But Bailey was the only one who said, "I felt it. You mean that warm spot?"

"Yes!" Becca said eagerly.

"It was something bad," Bailey said simply.

Becca thought for a moment. "Yes, it was!" she agreed.

"Now my grandchildren are losing it," Grandma said. She shook her head as if trying to get water out of her ears. "Now they think we're in a—a vortex or something! That pig is making everybody crazy!"

"Not a vortex, Grandma," Becca explained. "A warm wall." Although maybe it *was* a vortex— whatever that even was.

"Answer me this: What's the difference between a warm wall and a vortex?" Grandma frowned at Becca.

"Grandma, a vortex is something that whirls," K.C. chimed in. But Grandma frowned like she was about to scold him, so he added, "Never mind."

Anyway, past the wall now, Saucy burst into a run, and Becca trailed behind her, the air cool now against her face. They ran and ran. And ran!

And forgot about the warm wall.

CHAPTER FIFTEEN

SHINER

And even though none of them had said anything, it seemed Becca's brothers had missed her as she stayed in the kitchen each night. Or they missed the pig. Or both. Because one night she woke up to find them all in sleeping bags on the floor beside her. They were awake, Bailey on the other side of Saucy.

"K.C., I smell bleach. You didn't wipe it up good," Bailey was whispering. "It might bother Saucy."

Becca sniffed. She could vaguely smell bleach—bleach was Grandma's answer to everything. If any of the sinks got even a little stopped

up, she poured bleach in until the smell invaded
the entire house. If she saw you spill a speck of
food, she'd say, "Stop right there!" She'd put on
gloves and pour bleach on your minuscule mess
and then make you clean up the bleach. It didn't
matter that Mom had four other cleaners that
smelled better. Grandma only trusted bleach.
Earlier in the evening, Grandma had claimed to
smell something on the floor and had poured

bleach on it and let the bleach sit for an entire hour before telling K.C. to clean it up. Whenever Grandma told you to clean up her bleach, there was no arguing with her. You just did it and got on with your life.

Becca looked at her phone—it was three thirty in the morning!

"I had a big, new idea" was K.C.'s only reply to the bleach comment. "About the simulation." Of course that's what it was about! He paused, as if still considering his thoughts. Becca heard the fan whirring. She'd placed it right in front of the kitchen window, so it would blow cool air in.

"I was thinking maybe we ourselves—you know, humans—are all creating the simulation. We're, like, creating all these thoughts and ideas in our heads, all of us together. See, we form the simulation with all our wrong ideas and right ones too. We create each other and sometimes we, like, kill each other in wars or whatever. But it's *us*. *We're* creating it. In other words, it's not a video game someone created a million billion years ago. It's us, right now, altogether, creating the universe."

Becca tried to think about that, she really did. But it was a bit too heavy for her, especially at three thirty in the morning. So she just said politely, "That's a very good idea, K.C."

"Thank you."

"I don't get it," Jammer said, yawning. "The video game makes more sense . . . not that the video game makes much sense either." Then he added with a hint of outrage, "You know, I got a skate in three hours. Can you just think about the simulation instead of talking about it?" Then Becca saw him raise his head slightly, looking right at Saucy. "Good night."

Jammer was talking to Saucy, but K.C. and Bailey said, "Good night."

Bailey reached out and gave Saucy an affectionate pat before lying back down. "Saucy, come here!" Bailey cajoled.

But Saucy snuggled closer to Becca, lying half off her dog bed. Becca felt a little greedy, but she was glad Saucy stayed close to her.

When she woke up in the morning, however, Becca saw that Saucy was lying next to Bailey, not even on the dog bed anymore. He had his arms around her, and he was awake. He noticed her looking. "She's a good pig," he said. Well. That all made her happy and admittedly a little jealous. But mostly happy.

Saucy was still asleep, snoring. Becca remembered how when their cat had passed away, Bailey had been so upset Becca actually thought he might never stop crying. Their parents suggested a new cat; he'd said he never wanted another pet again.

But Bailey's face was shining now. Becca made an executive decision and resisted the urge to call Saucy over to her.

Usually Bailey liked to eat as soon as he was awake. But there they were in the kitchen, and he just lay there on the floor, cuddling with a pig. As Jammer left, Bailey smiled over at her. "Saucy reminds me of a cat, only different. She reminds me of *my* cat." He paused. "Shiner."

Their cat had been white, with a spot on his face like a black eye. That was why he was called Shiner. When Bailey would crawl along the floor, Shiner would walk slowly along beside him, never running ahead. Bailey hadn't mentioned his cat in ages, so long that Becca had thought he might have forgotten. But that was the thing about Bailey. He didn't forget things. He claimed he even remembered Grandpa. He said Grandpa smelled like pepper.

Becca's stomach growled. She really wanted to eat an apple and go take her shower, but if she moved, Saucy would get up and follow her. So she lay there. So that Bailey could hold a pig.

CHAPTER SIXTEEN
SIT, STAY, COME!

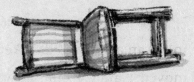

Saucy made snorty slurping noises when she ate her pellet feed. Becca thought the pellets looked gross, even for animal food, but they made Saucy *so* happy. Becca loved to watch her eat, because Saucy somehow managed to smile and eat at the same time. One morning Saucy ate for a bit, then stopped to look at Becca like she was grateful, like she still could remember her hungry, sick days, and then started eating again. She did this over and over.

Then Becca fed her chunks of vegetable and fruit, one piece at a time. She could have just put it all in a bowl and let Saucy gobble it down, but it was much more fun to feed her slowly. Saucy would delicately take each slice of cucumber or apple from Becca's fingers and eat it with little smacking sounds. When the bowl was empty, she looked eagerly and sweetly at Becca. Becca shook her head no. "More later, okay?" But apparently Saucy already knew what it meant when you shook your head no, and apparently "no" wasn't okay. Because she ran over to a kitchen chair and flipped it over, then turned to Becca and wagged her tail, all sweet again. And Becca gave in and let her have another few slices, because she was after all just a girl, not a real mom. A real mom knew how to say no.

Becca taught Saucy "sit," and Saucy was very good at it. You could say "sit" and *boom*, she was sitting. Though she occasionally listened to "come," she didn't always listen to "stay." That is, Becca was sure Saucy understood what "stay" meant, but she was just stubborn. She would stay when *she* wanted.

"You have to make her think it's *her* idea," Bailey explained as he watched one afternoon. "Here, let me show you." He looked at Saucy, who was sitting. "Saucy, don't you *want* to stay there? You want to stay there, right?" And he slowly scooted his butt backward along the floor. And Saucy stayed. "Come, Saucy!" he said triumphantly. But she stayed. "Saucy, don't *you* want to come? You don't have to, but don't you *want* to?" And Saucy came.

Becca was not at all sure Saucy wasn't trolling them, just to amuse herself. It must have been funny to see a bunch of eleven-year-old humans try to get her to "sit" and "stay" and "come," and then feed her cucumbers every time she knocked over a chair.

While everybody in the family paid attention

to Saucy, Becca could tell they knew it was *her* pig. It was just like how everybody had known Shiner was Bailey's cat. It was like even though she could tell Bailey wanted to spend more time with Saucy, he would sometimes reluctantly go play video games, just to leave Becca alone with her pig. Having her own pig made Becca feel better than she had since . . . well, since she found out she was a bad person inside. Now she felt like maybe she was kind of *good*. At least a little. After all, she made Saucy happy every day. She also felt like maybe she wasn't *ordinary*. After all, her pig was pretty *special*. *Extremely* special, in fact.

So like when she was walking home from the store later with four bags of fruits and vegetables, and she was pulling one of those goofy, vertical, two-wheeled grocery carts that belonged to Grandma, she didn't feel embarrassed at all when she ran into two girls from school and one of

them said, "A grocery cart?" and snickered. They were, in fact, two of the girls who had first told everyone to ignore MacKenzie.

Becca took a big breath and said proudly, "It's for my pet pig." The girls looked like they were on the verge of insulting her again.

But then one said, "Really? A pig? I like pigs."

And then they talked to her for ten minutes about Saucy. And invited themselves over to her house. When they came inside, they both immediately loved Saucy so much that Becca actually became a little alarmed and reminded them, "It's *my* pig." Because usually those girls got whatever they wanted.

Plus, they'd been so mean to MacKenzie. Well, so had she. Been mean. But not to *be* mean. That was different, right?

CHAPTER SEVENTEEN

CRISPY

Once Becca had decided not to weigh Saucy, she didn't for day after day after day. But then she had to do it anyway. Just to know. And Saucy had gained seventeen pounds. She now weighed forty-three. Which was actually impossible, or seemed like it should have been. Like how could pellets and vegetables have turned into seventeen pounds more pig so quickly?

One morning, as Saucy was in the backyard rummaging, K.C. opened a bag of salt-and-vinegar potato chips in the kitchen. And Saucy *blasted* into the house, ripping right through the sliding screen door! And knocked it out of its slot, so it wouldn't slide anymore. And *then* looked happily at K.C. like, *I, SAUCY, HAVE ARRIVED!*

She sat in front of him. She knew that they liked "sit." K.C. was holding a potato chip in the air near his mouth. Saucy grunted, as if to remind him that she was there. Her eyes were shining brightly, like *I'll wait right here for you to give me that chip! I know you're going to!*

K.C. lowered his hand, and she stood up on her back legs and took the chip. Then he gave her another: *smack, smack, smack.* "Don't give her too many," Becca scolded, like the world's biggest pig expert. "They aren't good for her."

But boy, Saucy *really* liked potato chips. It made K.C. smile. It made Becca smile. Even though Saucy was gaining weight even as they smiled.

But Becca had to fix the door. It took a lot of jiggling, but she got it back into the slot. She stepped back, evaluated. Maybe Mom and Dad wouldn't notice the big rip in the screen?

But of course they would. And did. And Becca knew it was bad. She knew this because they didn't say anything at all, just looked at each other in the same way they had that one time Bailey asked if he could hang around with a boy they didn't like. Nobody liked this boy, because he couldn't stop himself from being mean and, well, *bad*, but Bailey felt sad for him. And the boy came over, and afterward some money was missing from Mom's purse. And Mom and Dad had looked at each other that *way*. And *that* was how they looked at each other now. "I'll put it on my list of things I need to pay you back for," Becca quickly said. But she couldn't help adding, "How much total does Jammer's hockey gear cost?" Nobody replied. Silence.

But that night, as she, her brothers, and Saucy

all lay in the kitchen, she remembered the look her parents had given each other. That look made her hold extra tight to Saucy. "Do you think Mom and Dad were mad about the door?" she asked her brothers.

"Yeah," they all said immediately.

That made her hold even tighter, until Saucy squirmed, and she loosened her grip. Her cheek lay against the back of Saucy's head. Piglet hair wasn't fuzzy or soft. It still surprised Becca that it felt crispy, like a towel that had been hung on the line instead of put into the dryer. Saucy's ears were like that too, crispy. Becca loved Saucy's ears, she loved them! They smelled a little like dirt, and a little bit piggy. Becca had washed her again today, with the special shampoo, so she didn't smell quite as piggy as usual. Washing her, however, was not something she wanted to think about. She'd tried it outside. It had not gone well, and had involved Saucy running headlong into the wooden fence. For no apparent reason. Which had made them both scream. At least nobody had called the police this time.

Saucy was snoring lightly. So was Bailey. Very peaceful. K.C. and Jammer always slept like rocks and almost never made any noise at all, except for one time last year when Jammer had yelled out, "Dillon!" That was a boy on his team who never passed to anyone unless you yelled at him. That had made her realize that Jam thought about hockey nonstop not only when he was awake, but when he was asleep, too. Just like all she ever thought about now was pigs in general, and her pig in particular. And K.C. thought about the simulation, and Bailey about his music. She felt like she really understood her brothers now, like *really* understood them. And all because she had a pig.

She suddenly remembered she had not been taking her nightly selfies ever since she got Saucy. So she took one now, trying to fit everyone into the frame. She couldn't stop staring at the picture she had just taken. It was her favorite selfie, ever.

CHAPTER EIGHTEEN

A GOOD LIFE

In the morning, Becca woke to see Mom feeding *her* pig. Becca scrambled up from the floor. "But Mom? Shouldn't I be the one who feeds Saucy? Since she's my pig and everything?"

"We're bonding," Mom said. But then she also said, "Sweetheart . . ."

Becca didn't like the way she said that. Not at all.

Bailey coughed lightly, then said, "Bec, we *want* Mom to bond with Saucy."

"I like this pig," Mom said. She coughed lightly herself. "You love this pig. Bailey does too. Your other brothers even like her. Your father likes her. Your grandmother—well, who knows what she thinks? But it might be a good idea to, you know, just take her down to that sanctuary the veterinarian had mentioned, just to meet the other pigs. For no other reason! Okay? She's growing so fast. Let her get used to where she'll live someday. Okay? She needs a good life. We both agree on that, don't we?"

"She has a good life here!" Becca shouted.

"She has a good life," Bailey repeated calmly. "Mom, she does."

"She does, for the moment. But what about when she's hundreds of pounds and you're all in school? She'll be lonely, and think of what she'll be able to destroy by that time."

Becca did think about it sometimes. She thought about the couch, which was kind of expensive just because it was so big. But she didn't think it was massively expensive, at least for a couch. And anyway, Saucy might be able to destroy some cushions, but would she really be able to destroy the entire couch? There was also the refrigerator. She was pretty sure that was one of the most expensive things they owned, just because it made ice, which couldn't be easy. Their old fridge hadn't made ice. Also, it was big, and big things usually cost more. But what else was there that it would be a big deal if Saucy destroyed?

"But Mom . . ." Becca heard whininess in her voice. Mom always said not to whine. So she cleared her throat and repeated, "Mom" more firmly. "She's still small. You said a hundred pounds."

"I said a hundred, *maybe* sixty. But I didn't realize how . . . destructive she'd be. Or the amount she eats, which is fine, but at the same time, honey, you knew we couldn't keep her forever. Let's do this with as little disruption to

Saucy as possible. Let's start getting her used to her future home. Just a visit. Okay? For Saucy?"

Becca felt her face grow hot. She was sure it was red, too. "You're trying to manipulate me!" she said accusingly. "By saying it's all for Saucy and not because you're mad that she's broken things! And Mom, I'm going to make everything up to you! Someday I'm going to pay you back for everything she's wrecked!" "You're trying to manipulate me" was a line her parents used sometimes on her and her brothers. Which for sure they tried to do sometimes, because sometimes you kind of *had* to! Otherwise you wouldn't get your way!

"I called the sanctuary yesterday. They sounded *very* nice," Mom persisted. "We're going to make them a donation, and when the time comes—not now, but eventually—they'll take her. Okay?"

Was Mom *crazy*? Had Mom lost her *mind*? Giving Saucy to the sanctuary was way, way, *way* in the future! That was many, many pounds away. Because Mom *had* said one hundred, at first. She had, and everybody had heard her!

"Just yesterday, your father was reading that pigs really enjoy having another pig in their life. Can you imagine how lonely it might be for a pig without another one around?"

Mom was trying to manipulate her again, but Becca ignored that. "Then why can't we get another pig?" she asked. "Then Saucy will have a friend while I'm at school."

"Bec, come on, you know why."

In fact, Becca did know why—because two pigs would eventually be twelve hundred total pounds of pig. Which would be twelve hundred pounds of destructive force. Which was a lot. If about forty pounds of pig could destroy cabinets, curtains, and screen doors, it was hard to even imagine what twelve hundred pounds could do. She thought about Bailey crawling on the floor, and two giant pigs running into him. That would pretty much be the worst thing that could happen to their family.

So she didn't argue anymore. In fact, she didn't even feel like arguing. She just felt so sad. Later that day, after Saucy's breakfast, and after the family's breakfast, the leftovers of which became Saucy's extra breakfast, Becca put Saucy's harness on. It was a new one, made just for pigs, because Saucy had gotten too big for the first one Dad had bought. As usual, Saucy twirled and then did zoomies in her harness, because she was just so darned excited to go for a walk.

Then Saucy stopped her zoomies suddenly. Becca knew it was because she knew something was up. It would be hard to explain to someone who didn't know a pig just how smart they were, and the *way* they were smart.

For instance, Saucy did this thing sometimes where she would go "hahahahaha" in a somewhat deeper voice than her usual squeal. The interesting thing was, Saucy didn't say "hahahahaha" when she thought something was funny, but when she thought *they* thought something was funny. It was hard to explain. She was a very smart pig. Dad said one night, "This pig understands things you wouldn't think a pig would understand . . . not that I know a lot about what pigs understand."

Anyway, now she stopped her zoomies and ran up to each of them one by one, wagging her tail very slightly and judging them. She liked to judge them. That was hard to explain too. She was a very judgmental little pig. She liked Becca best, then Bailey, then a tie between Jammer and K.C.

She kind of liked Mom and Dad, but she sometimes pretended to like them more than she did,
because she knew they were in charge. Anyway,
that was how Becca figured it. And Saucy ignored
Grandma, except to look at her sometimes and
make a judging noise like "hmmmm."

Now Becca had to tug a little harder than
usual before Saucy would go outside, because she
was too busy judging them. "We're going to have
fun, Saucy! It's going to be so much fun!" Then
she felt guilty, because she truthfully had no idea
if it would be fun at all.

Saucy didn't like the ramp that Bailey used
for his wheelchair; for some reason, it scared her.
Jammer was the strongest, so he lifted Saucy into
the van. Even Grandma had decided to come to
the sanctuary. It would be all of them except Dad,
because he was at work. He was working an extra
lot lately. Becca had a terrible thought: Maybe he

160

was working harder to pay for everything the pig was breaking? Plus, there was the animal hospital bill. Plus, apparently, a donation to this sanctuary place. Plus, Saucy ate a really lot of food. Like more food than you could imagine someone about forty pounds could eat. Even if that someone was a pig. Even if you weren't sure precisely how much this pig weighed that day.

Becca suddenly felt so worried that she kept gagging in the car, like she wanted to throw up. She didn't know what to expect at the sanctuary, on top of which she didn't really want to see where Saucy might live someday. *Would* live someday.

Mom was driving into the countryside, curving through woods and emerging into farmland. Finally she pulled over at a place with a sign that said PEACEFUL PIG SANCTUARY. They sat in the car for a full minute, nobody moving. Just studying the sanctuary. It was big. It had grass. It had dirt and mud. It had smiling people. It had So. Many. Pigs! There were black pigs and pink pigs, spotted pigs and brown pigs. And one gray pig. There were pigs lying in the grass; pigs relaxing in the mud; pigs digging; pigs "talking" to humans. Big pigs, little pigs, in-between pigs. And all of them looked very, very happy. In the car, Saucy's hooves were on the window. She was whining and squealing. So Becca leashed her and got out, Saucy spilling down and pulling Becca to a fence, snorting wildly. The rest of the family chased after them. Saucy stood at the wood fence, twirling and staring, staring and twirling, the leash getting all tangled.

Becca spotted a gate. "Come on, Saucy!" She hauled her pig over to the gate and unlatched it, pausing to look back. Her brothers and Mom were hurrying over too, as if Becca had also called *them*.

"What about waiting for an old woman!" Grandma scolded loudly, bringing up the rear. "I gave birth to your father, you know!"

Once Grandma caught up, Becca unleashed Saucy . . . and created bedlam! Saucy dashed right in, and it seemed like some of the pigs absolutely LOVED her, and some of them already HATED her. Pigs were running around everywhere! One of them ran up and butted Becca in the legs!

Saucy was instantly furious, half screaming and half snarling at the head-butter, even though the other pig was full-grown.

A woman rushed up out of nowhere crying out, "No, no, no!" She held Saucy's face in her hands and tilted her head, saying, "Honey, honey, honey. It's okay. Who are you?" She asked that directly to Saucy, not to Becca or her family. Saucy magically calmed down. "I'm at one with the pigs," the woman said confidently.

Another pig came up to touch noses with Saucy. The others, thankfully, had calmed down when the woman arrived. "This is Saucy," Becca told her.

"I called the sanctuary earlier to say we were coming to visit," Mom added.

"Yes, I remember. I spoke with you." She leaned in and kissed Saucy's nose. "What a cutie!"

Saucy looked so pleased that jealousy pinged

through Becca. The woman began to have a whole conversation with Saucy and the other pig. "Now are you two going to get along if I let Saucy go free? I would really appreciate it if you would do that. What do you say? Do you think you could do that?"

They both looked at her innocently. Saucy even sat. So the woman stepped back, after which Saucy and her new friend simply walked off together, as if to talk privately. Next they chased each other around for a couple of minutes, and then lay in the sun for what seemed like forever.

The woman, who'd been nodding at the two pigs, said, "I'm Lady, and yes that's my real name. I run this place three days a week, spend the night here, even. Most everybody is a volunteer, but there are five of us on salary, and two of us are here at all times. Feel free to ask me whatever you'd like."

She put out her hand and shook each of theirs in turn. But when she put out her hand to Grandma, Grandma didn't put out hers. Then the woman put hers down, and Grandma put out hers. Finally they shook. You never knew if Grandma did stuff like that on purpose, but probably she did.

"Do you only have pigs here?" Becca asked.

"We started out pig only, but every so often someone begs us to please take an animal that will be killed otherwise. So we have a couple of goats, and three dogs. We even have a llama." She snorted—not loudly, but it was definitely a snort.

To be honest, Becca thought the woman seemed a little, well, wacky. Not completely wacky, but for sure a little. In a nice way. Not in a bad way. Like there was something pig-like about her. Or if not piglike, not altogether human. Kind of like the woman they got Shiner from years ago. That woman said that in the previous nine years she had placed nine thousand cats in homes.

That led Becca to a disturbing thought. "You wouldn't try to place Saucy with a home, would you? I mean, what if you did that and they . . . well . . . ate her?" And now Becca's lower lip began to tremble, and she wasn't sure she could get it to stop. It seemed like her lower lip was entirely separate from her brain!

"We do place the mini-pigs sometimes, but it's very hard to find them homes. With the farm pigs, we have placed a few, but never to be eaten. The new owners have to sign a form that the animal won't be put down prematurely for any reason."

That disturbed Becca even more, because just the thought . . . it was awful! "But what if they lie?" She had met quite a few liars in her life. There were certain kids at school who lied for no reason at all. Just because they felt like it.

"We could give you a substantial donation," Mom said. "That is, if you promised never to place Saucy. She's my daughter's pig."

Becca wondered how much money they had in savings. She felt guilty for a brief moment that she was costing so much money, but then she blurted out, "Yes, we'll give you all the money we have!"

Lady took Becca's hand and seemed to look straight into her soul. "I'm sure we can work something out. Nobody is going to hurt your pig, I promise."

"But what if you're lying?" Becca couldn't help but asking. She closed her eyes tightly as tears squeezed out.

"I *never* lie," Lady said sternly. "The last time I lied was seven years ago, but that was a harmless white lie when my sister got a bad haircut, and I told her it was cute. I still remember that, because I *never* lie." And she did the snorting thing again.

Someone was calling out, "Lady, that new pig with three legs just vomited!"

"Oh!" Lady exclaimed as she rushed off.

They decided to sit on some benches and watch the pigs, except for Grandma and Bailey. Bailey was making a slow circle on the grass near the benches. He made circles sometimes when he was thinking. For some reason Grandma started wandering around among the pigs, as if she were in some kind of pig museum. Sometimes she lingered and studied a pig like it was an interesting painting or sculpture.

A spotted pig came up to the benches and began studying them, as if *they* were sculptures. Becca had the thought that the spotted pig was part of the simulation. Then it walked off.

But all of a sudden Saucy looked up in a

panic, spotted Becca, and scampered over, full of relief to see her. Her hooves thumped the dirt over and over, raising little clouds of dust. Then she launched herself into the air and landed on Becca's lap, nearly knocking her back off the bench. Then she slipped back to the ground and looked toward the gate, back to Becca, and back to the gate.

"She wants to go home," Bailey said.

Lady was nowhere to be seen, probably dealing with the three-legged, vomiting pig. So Mom said they should just go home, and maybe bring Saucy back every few days for visits with her new friend.

"I don't think that's a good idea," Becca said. Everybody looked at her expectantly, so she continued. "This place is a little wacky."

"Of course it's wacky," Bailey said, laughing. "It's a bunch of pigs. They're probably all crazy, just like Saucy. And then the people who spend all their time with them are going to get a little crazy too. That's all. I like it here! This place is *great*."

It seemed as if Saucy had had a lot of fun at the sanctuary, but also that she was perfectly happy to leave. And she twirled about twenty times in the kitchen when she got home. Just from the sheer joy of being back where she belonged— Becca could tell. But for the rest of the day, Becca had a pain in her stomach. And then during dinner, Saucy seemed exhausted. She had played a lot with the other pig, but she also seemed *emotionally* exhausted. She was a very emotional pig! Her eyes fluttered sleepily right in the middle of dinner.

When Becca and her brothers lay on the floor for bed, Saucy had already been asleep for an hour. Nobody spoke, Jammer and K.C. on their phones, Becca and Bailey staring into space.

"It's all good," Bailey finally said. "The sanctuary will be a good life for her." Becca looked at him, saw he was about to cry. He saw her looking and pulled the sleeping bag over his face.

Becca didn't answer, just listened to Saucy snoring. Some of her snores sounded like they should be coming from a much bigger pig, but then she settled down into tiny baby snores. Pig snoring was pretty much the greatest sound in the world.

CHAPTER NINETEEN

GAINING WEIGHT

A few days later, Bailey had the crazy idea that they should bring Saucy to the rink because (1) she would be amazed to see Jammer skate, (2) they could show her off to new people, and (3) she might like the cool air.

So they did. She was the center of attention, wrapped in a heavy blanket—the rink was *cold*— and leaning lovingly against Becca in the bleachers. Nearly every person there came by at some point to say hello, and Saucy seemed to love the attention. But then out of the blue she got quite angry when one man reached out to pet her. First she barked and made a noise that approached a

growl. Then she even snapped at him and would have bitten him if he hadn't quickly drawn his hand away. She'd never acted like that before!

So Becca had to take her outside to wait in the hot sun until Jammer finished skating. They sat against a wall in the semi-shade, watching the hockey kids carry their sticks and big bags inside, and other hockey kids carry their sticks and big bags outside and heave them into cars. Saucy was panting by the time Jammer finished his skate.

But just as they were walking to the van, somebody passed by walking a terrier puppy. Saucy got furious! She lunged toward the sidewalk, pulling Becca over, barking and snarling like the meanest dog you could imagine. Jammer lunged after them, grabbed the leash with Becca, and then K.C. joined, and together they pulled the pig back to the van . . . where she calmed down and instantly smiled up at them sweetly.

Jammer lifted Saucy into the van with a grunt. "She's getting heavy," he commented. He frowned. "In a few weeks, Bec, I might not be able to lift her anymore."

Saucy was now fifty-five pounds. In a month, she might weigh a hun— NO, Becca wasn't going to think about that. But Jammer was. His forehead was getting wrinkly. Then he looked determined. "But I might be able to lift her for a long time. I might." He looked suddenly defiant as he slid into the van. "Yeah, I'll be able to lift her for another two or three months."

But Becca knew there was something that would be even better, in terms of being able to keep Saucy longer. She looked at K.C. "So do you think I can control the simulation to stop Saucy from growing?" She felt inspired by how determined Jammer was. She would be just as determined: she would control the simulation!

"You can try it," K.C. said. "It'd be an interesting experiment."

So the whole ride home, Becca concentrated on stopping Saucy from growing.

And yet every day Saucy gained another pound, sometimes two. There was one day when she gained *three*. How was that even possible?

And what could Becca do? She couldn't stop feeding her. She tried sitting on her ragged zafu for an entire hour one morning, concentrating on controlling the simulation. Then she weighed Saucy, who'd gained three pounds *again*.

"It's your simulation—*you* change it!" she half yelled at K.C.

Seeing how sad he got after she said that made Becca feel guilty over how she sometimes thought she loved Saucy most of everybody, because she actually loved K.C. a lot too. And Bailey. And *even* Jammer—she loved him a whole lot! And Mom and Dad. Grandma—yes, she even loved Grandma. But . . . still, none of them was Saucy.

CHAPTER TWENTY

THE LAST WALK

One Friday in August, Becca and her brothers washed Saucy outside together. Becca hadn't weighed her recently, but she was getting too heavy to lift in and out of the tub.

Saucy stood glumly on the concrete. Jammer leaned over her, holding tightly, getting soaked as K.C. sprayed the hose and Becca soaped up Saucy's hair. If Becca didn't think about the weight gain, she loved soaping Saucy's growing belly. It just felt so *piggy* and healthy. Saucy was no longer thin and frail like when they'd found her. Becca felt so, so proud of how well she was taking care of her pig!

Bailey sat back a ways so as not to get his wheelchair wet. But he bossed them around quite a bit, yelling out things like "Becca, you missed a spot!" Or, "Jam, let Becca get that place under Saucy's tail!"

Instead of her usual screaming, Saucy was making a very high-pitched humming noise. She sounded like—like she was trapped in a well and had been crying out for hours, and now was so tired she could only hum.

At last Becca cried out, "There! I'm done!"

K.C. sprayed the soap off as Jammer held Saucy still. Jam got as wet as Saucy!

When he let go, Saucy ran around and around the yard, still humming. Finally she lay down on the concrete, panting. They all went over to comfort her. Bailey even climbed out of his chair to sit next to her. "It's okay, piggy, it's okay," he murmured. Just like he used to say, "It's okay, kitty" to Shiner.

Then, out of *nowhere*, Dad came out back and said *extremely* suddenly, and for *no* reason, "I guess it's time to take Saucy on her last family walk."

And, okay, it wasn't out of *nowhere*. Because that morning Saucy had done her worst thing ever: bitten Mom when Mom tried to push her away from the garden she was rebuilding.

"Dad, she's not a hundred pounds!" Becca screamed. It just came out of her mouth as a scream! "Not nearly!" she added.

"Bec," Dad said solemnly. "You know what this is about."

"That was Mom's fault! She tried to make her leave the garden! Saucy loves the garden!" Becca was shouting at her dad louder than she'd ever before shouted at one of her parents, except for earlier that day after Saucy bit Mom, and she shouted, "MOM, THAT WASN'T HER FAULT!"

"Becca," Dad said seriously. "Your mom loves the garden, and whose fault would you say it was? There's no excuse for biting." For once, he hadn't spoken in clichés.

"But Dad, she's a *pig*. I don't understand why Mom has to garden *now*. Why can't she garden after—after Saucy has . . . gone to the sanctuary?"

Dad knelt down and rubbed Saucy's tummy. Saucy liked that so much that she turned all the way on her back and kicked her hooves into the air, humming with satisfaction. "Everything happens for a reason," Dad said. "You saved this pig's life. And now it's time to, uh . . . It's better to have loved and lost than never to have loved at all. I believe that." Back to the clichés—this seemed like a good sign, for sure better than how serious he'd been a moment earlier.

"What about my cat?" Bailey asked. "Was it better to have loved my cat than never to have loved him at all?" But then he immediately added, "Never mind, it was better, I agree." He turned to Becca. "I agree with him, Bec."

Becca was staring at Bailey. "You're supposed to be on *my* side!"

Bailey looked sincerely surprised. "I'm on everybody's side," he said, as if that were obvious. This was true. Bailey loved everybody; he was truly on everybody's side. Unlike herself.

Becca stared at the ground. She felt like wrapping her arms around her pig and never letting go. But she also felt like if she moved, she might start crying and never stop. Instead she concentrated on staying very still. Saucy gave out a little bark and jumped to her feet. She knew something was wrong. She stuck her nose toward Dad and went "Hmmmm. Hmmmmm." Judging him.

"I'm here!" Grandma announced, causing

them all to look at her. She looked furious. Then she said, "This is an outrage! She loves that pig!"

What? Grandma was on Becca's side!

"We can't keep a six-hundred-pound biting pig," Dad stated firmly. "Are you going to take care of this pig, Mother? You have a bad back. What if she bites *you*?"

"Many people have pigs for pets. I looked it up!" Becca said.

"They're mini-pigs," K.C. corrected her. "And they're not even that mini. Never mind, I don't want to get involved."

Bailey was sitting with his fingers in his ears and his eyes closed. Jammer, who'd been stick-handling a puck, paused worriedly.

Grandma clapped her hands together loudly. "Listen to me, everybody listen to me. For goodness' sake, I'll take care of the pig while Becca's in school!"

But even though Becca wanted to, she couldn't even get excited by those words. Because she knew. She knew that Grandma could not care for a six-hundred-pound pig. She also knew that a six-hundred-pound pig should not live in a house with a small yard. She knew that, for whatever reason, the simulation had put a pig into her life and was also going to take it away. If this *was* a simulation. Regardless, she was not in control. They all knew that. That was why nobody said anything else, because what could any of them say?

So she stood up, crying, and announced bravely, "I'll put on her harness."

Becca wanted to take the route that went by where they had found Saucy, even though that was where the creepy, warm feeling was. So that was what they did. They left late, to give the night a chance to cool off.

Becca cried every step, and nobody else said a single thing. K.C. wore his earbuds the whole time. Totally against the rules, because their parents wanted everybody to "interact" and "engage" during these walks. But nobody said a word about that, either. It was the quietest walk ever, except for the clitter-clatter of Saucy's hooves. The moon cast a glow on her back. She really was the most perfect pig in the world, Becca thought gratefully. She had gotten to live with a perfect pig for weeks. That was the good news. Pretty much everything else was bad. At the moment, anyway.

When they got to the warm, creepy place, Saucy snorted and whined. Then she whirled around and got the leash tangled, which was what she did when she wanted to be let off leash. As Becca paused to straighten things out, Saucy lunged forward, twisting the leash out of Becca's

hands, then just about *smashed* straight into the bushes, in pretty much the exact spot where Becca had found her!

Saucy snorted and pawed, branches snapping and cracking, until only her tail was sticking out. Grasping Saucy's back legs, Becca finally managed to pull her out. But now there was a big hole in the bushes. Yikes! The owner would be mad! She started to patch it up. But an odd, sick smell was wafting into her nose. She handed Saucy's leash to Jammer, then peered into the hole.

And saw another world.

That is . . . it was part of this world. But it wasn't. Most everything was just a big, empty field. But in the distance was a line of long, long windowless buildings. There were no people, no trees, no pretty plants—just those long, eerily lit buildings. Nine of them. The smell made her gag, and she turned to the side and spit into the grass.

"What're ya doing, Bec?" Bailey asked.

She pulled her head away from the hole. "Mom, Dad, look!"

Then one by one her entire family looked through the branches. First Mom and Dad. Then Bailey crawled down to see. Her other brothers. And with a huge grunt, Grandma herself peered through the hole.

"What is all that back there?" Bailey asked as he crawled back to his chair. He could pull himself back up sometimes, but right now he glanced at Jammer, his signal that he wanted Jammer's help. Jammer lifted him into the chair. Jam's face was dirty for some reason. Saucy was sitting in front of Dad, as if waiting for an explanation.

"It must be a farm," Dad said.

"That's no farm!" Grandma scoffed. "I grew up on a farm, or did you forget that?"

"A *factory* farm," Dad clarified. "I've seen pictures of them." He looked suddenly at Saucy. "Oh!"

Becca instantly understood. "It's a pig farm! Pigs live inside those buildings!" Pure panic flooded her entire being. "Let's get out of here!" What if someone found them with Saucy?!

"Becca!" her mother cried, but Becca had grabbed the leash from Jammer and was already running as fast as she could. She ran and ran until she was too tired to continue. Then with a grunt, she tried to scoop Saucy up, but could only heave her a couple of feet in the air, then had to set her down.

The rest of the family caught up except for Jammer, who trailed behind, hands in his pockets, as he whistled innocently. Then he said to Becca in a low voice, "I tried to fill in the hole in the bushes. I don't know why, just thought I should. In case someone noticed the hole and came after Saucy. I mean, or something. I don't know."

CHAPTER TWENTY-ONE
SANCTUARY

Actually, Becca now wanted to take Saucy to the sanctuary right that minute. What if "they" caught her with one of their pigs? What if *they* heard she had a pig? Even though Saucy was now *her* pig? *They* could find out—maybe they already knew! Becca had looked up "sanctuary" in the dictionary. It was a sacred place where you had immunity. Saucy would be safe there!

Mom and Dad convinced her that the morning would be fine for taking Saucy to safety. "Why don't you have one more night with your pig?" Dad said. "That's the way it should be."

So when they got home, Becca made sure all

the doors and windows were locked. But as she lay with her brothers on the kitchen floor, she didn't feel entirely *right*. So she got up and went to her parents' room, knocking first and then walking in before they answered.

"Mom? Dad? Are you awake?"

"Yes, what is it?" they both asked at the same time.

"I think you should come sleep on the kitchen floor too, since this is Saucy's last night."

Her parents didn't answer at first. Then Dad silently picked up his pillow, grabbed his robe, and walked out—apparently to the kitchen. Mom sighed but said, "Okay, honey." She too grabbed her pillow and robe.

Becca followed her mom. When they got to the kitchen, Dad was already lying down, his head on the pillow and the robe covering him like a blanket. Becca's brothers were watching their parents with blank faces, but they were the kind of blank faces that were only pretending to be blank and really meant, *Huh? What's going on?*

"Dad, don't you want your sleeping bag?" Becca asked.

"It's in the garage," he replied. "I don't feel like looking for it. I'll live. What doesn't kill you makes you stronger." He said that as if he was trying to convince himself that he was getting stronger at this very moment.

Mom was looking doubtfully at the floor. She sighed again and lay down. "Mom, you can use my sleeping bag," Becca said.

"I'll be fine. You be comfortable next to your pig. This is *your* night. Although, honey, if you wouldn't mind grabbing me a sheet from the closet? I can't sleep under nothing."

Becca went to get the sheet, Saucy following

her to the closet and back again to the kitchen, then lying down on her psychedelic bed.

Becca was up for a long time, listening to the crickets outside. She thought about how just a couple of months ago, she was an ordinary, normal girl without a pig. Now she was special. She wondered if she would go back to being ordinary after Saucy was gone. That is, if you'd been special for a while, did it "stick"? She felt like her insides were some kind of lonely, sick goo.

And yet she knew that Saucy would be fine at the sanctuary. She just knew it.

And *yet* here she was stressed anyway. She remembered a night, just before Christmas, when MacKenzie had called and left her a message. She could tell from MacKenzie's voice that her insides were a lonely, sick goo. MacKenzie hadn't had three brothers, a mom, and a dad to sleep on the floor with her. She hadn't had a pig. Becca could not even imagine feeling the way she felt at this moment, and not having any of those people—and a pig—around her. Although, after a bit of concentration, she *could* imagine it. She *could* imagine how lonely and desperate MacKenzie must have felt to call Becca, who had abandoned her, who had not spoken to her for months.

A couple of days before MacKenzie's mom had been arrested, when Becca had slept over that night, the pancakes Mac's mom had made them were chocolate chip. Organic, with organic syrup, because they were a healthy family that way. MacKenzie's mom did not want any chemicals in anyone's bodies. She used to say to Becca that she wanted her to be healthy her whole life. Ha-ha, every Christmas she used to give Becca and her brothers each a bottle of organic vitamin C gummies. Just because she cared. It didn't make sense that she had broken the law in a big enough way that she had to go to jail. In fact, that was the first time that Becca had seriously considered whether she might be living in a simulation, where some kind of alien was randomly making things happen that were completely illogical. Making stuff happen for no other reason than just because. How else to make sense of someone you know making you pancakes, and then getting arrested two days later? How else to make sense of finding a pig on the road and falling in love with it? How else to make sense of Dad sleeping on the floor under his robe when he had to go to work tomorrow for a client? Even though tomorrow was Saturday. Becca thought of all the things he had to pay for.

She slept then, she thought, but she wasn't sure. She was kind of sleeping and kind of not, and the next thing she knew, Grandma was standing over them saying, "My son sleeping on the floor

with his wife and a pig. I told you this pig was making the whole family crazy! I told you, didn't I?" She paused. "But we should still keep it."

Becca decided that they should have some kind of special good-bye breakfast. Everyone picked out a vegetable or fruit to feed Saucy. She, Jammer, and K.C. chose avocado, because Saucy loved that so much, but Bailey chose cucumbers, because he wanted her to remember him especially. Mom and Dad decided on apples, and Grandma chose pellets for the vitamins in them.

They all sat in a circle around Saucy, who wore an excited expression, like she couldn't believe this was happening. All the good food! All the attention! She snorted and chomped and smacked. And smiled.

It was a ritual, a sacred good-bye ritual. And it made Saucy so happy! When you saw a pig that happy, all you could do was smile. You couldn't cry at all, even if you were about to give your pig to a sanctuary.

Then Dad said, "Becca, I told the sanctuary we would be there by nine thirty. We can't stay too long. Remember, I have a client coming into the office and need to get to work by noon." He paused. "I'm sorry, Bec. I'm real sorry. I know this is going to be a hard day for you." More pausing. "But what doesn't kill you . . ."

So they all got dressed without even eating breakfast themselves. Becca's stomach was rumbling with hunger. Or was just sick and gooey. She couldn't really tell. Anyway, her stomach was messed up. They went outside and piled into the van. Saucy was in her harness, sitting in Becca's lap—Jammer had lifted her up and set her down. Becca had to admit that it was very uncomfortable. But she loved to see Saucy smiling as she looked out the window. This would be the last time they would ride together in the van.

K.C. looked over at her and Saucy. "See, here's what I don't understand about time," he said. "We're here, and usually when you're *here*, in the present, that's just where you are. The present is the most powerful. But sometimes the future feels more powerful. Like right now. So even though we're here in the present, are we also kind of in the future?"

Becca felt a very slight sensation of that possibly making sense to her.

Jammer, however, looked at him with a slightly exasperated expression, like *Whatever, K.C.* Probably they were all thinking that. But Jammer was the only one who showed it.

They saw a dog at a stoplight, and Saucy went, "Hmmmm." Judging the dog. Then she barked. Then they started moving forward again.

Grandma was saying, "I don't know why everybody thinks I'm too old to take care of a pig. You know, I gave birth three times. That's harder than taking care of a pig."

"Can I just say, Mom? You were . . . younger then," Dad said.

SAUCY

For once Grandma didn't talk back. That was probably because in her heart she knew she was too old to take care of a six-hundred-pound pig. Even though the pig was only sixty pounds at the moment. Or sixty-two. Or maybe even sixty-five. Becca wondered what it would feel like to have a six-hundred-pound pig in her lap. Could she even survive it? But maybe the important point right now was that Grandma for sure couldn't survive it if a six-hundred-pound pig tried to sit on her. Which you never knew, Saucy might try, just because she was a little unpredictable.

When they arrived at the sanctuary, Becca let Saucy run without the leash to the gate. She wanted to shout, "Be free!" She remembered that movie *Born Free*, which she watched three nights in a row last year and cried every time. It was about a lioness named Elsa. Elsa was born free, and then tamed, and then set free again to live the way she was meant to live. It was kind of the same as their situation, wasn't it? Except Saucy was born in captivity, became a pet, and now was going to live the way she was meant to. Becca had loved that movie *so much*. That was because something really similar had been in her future. Anyway, K.C. might say that.

So she flung open the gate and shouted, "Be free, Saucy!" And Saucy snorted and ran happily in. Just like Elsa would have if Elsa had been a pig!

Lady was already approaching them.

"So here's the royal princess!" Lady said cheerfully. "What a cutie!" She smiled brightly.

But nobody else smiled. They all went through the gate, and Becca saw Mom hand Lady a piece of paper, probably a check for a donation. "How much is it?" she asked her mother, trying to peek.

"It doesn't matter."

"But how much?"

"Well . . . three thousand dollars. It's a donation. That's how these sanctuaries survive."

"We wanted to make sure Saucy was well taken care of," Dad said firmly. He looked at Becca. "And that they wouldn't adopt her out to someone who might end up, you know . . . doing anything that would make her not able to be your pig anymore because, uh . . ."

Three thousand dollars! On the one hand, that was a lot of money. On the other hand, Saucy was worth at least ten million!

Dad said to Lady, "The kids really love the pig, but it's challenging having her around the house."

"Of course," Lady said. "I understand completely. I love every single one of these pigs." She spoke quite fervently, giving Becca hope that Saucy would have a lovely life here. Lady laughed. "Even when they bite me, I still love them."

Then she started talking about sharing the planet with all the pigs and all the animals, and how she even loved sea creatures and liked to just watch videos on YouTube of octopuses changing colors, and fish swimming in the depth of the sea, and . . . She talked for a long time, even though all Becca really wanted to hear about was how well she would be taking care of Saucy. "But I see your eyes glazing over," she suddenly said to Becca. She laughed again. "I'm very direct! It comes from hanging around with pigs all day!" She walked off without another word.

They sat on the benches for an hour watching Saucy lounge around, digging a bit by herself before lying in the sun with the same pig from her last visit. Then Becca saw Dad checking the time on his phone. He and Mom glanced at each other. So Becca knew that it was time to go. She stared down at her lap. She had a weird sensation, like all of a sudden she was imagining herself as a pig too, like she wanted to eat some fruit and kale and dig a hole in the dirt. At the moment, she would rather be a pig than Becca.

Dad and Mom stood up. Becca and her brothers didn't. Then, one by one, they did, except for Bailey, who was doing circles.

A woman Becca hadn't seen before came up and said, "You're Becca, right? We'll take good care of your pig, I promise. She's already one of my favorites. What a happy girl she is!" She paused. "But maybe I should just take her away now. So she doesn't see you leave? That's the way I personally always do it." She glanced around. "Lady doesn't do it that way. She thinks it causes less anxiety in the long run for the pig to know exactly what's going on."

Everyone looked at Becca, and she said meekly, "Okay." Even though she wanted to run through the field and hug Saucy good-bye.

"Of course, you can come back as often as you want to visit Saucy. Okay? All right? We had one person who came back every day at first." She took Becca's hands in hers. "My family had to give away a dog once, because our apartment wouldn't let us have her. It was hard, but we found a great home for her. It was a house with a yard. So I just . . . I cried a lot. But I was happy for her, and I know you'll be happy for Saucy, because she'll have everything she needs here, and we'll all love her, and she'll have all the pig friends she wants—or only a couple of friends if she prefers it that way. And she'll *always* remember you, because pigs are like that. Okay?"

Becca nodded, but the tears were already flowing. Then she watched Saucy being led away. When she was out of sight, they returned to the van. As soon as Dad turned on the ignition, Becca rolled down the window, because she could hear it. *Screaming!* Hysterical screaming. Saucy had heard the van start and knew what it meant!

"Let me out!" Becca shouted. She grasped at her hair and felt so crazy she wanted to pull it out. "NOW!"

But Dad put the van in reverse, saying, "Let's see how she does. I'll call the sanctuary later to make sure all's well that ends well. I promise!" And he backed out with a screech.

So it was good-bye, Saucy! *For now!*

All the way home, like every three minutes, Dad repeated, "I'll call them later to make sure she's okay."

Mom was dabbing away tears. Grandma kept muttering, "For Pete's sake, the factory farmer's not going to find her. They don't care! She's just one little pig. We should keep her another week at least! She's just a baby!"

"Grandma, we can't take a chance!" Becca exclaimed between choking sobs. "If I have to give her to the sanctuary anyway, I would rather do it now. I don't want to take a chance that the farmer might find out about her. The farmer might send the police!"

"A farmer isn't in charge of the police!" Grandma exclaimed back. "Who becomes a police officer to chase down baby pigs?"

"But there are the other things," Becca said, choking up.

"What other things?" Grandma demanded.

"The forty-nine things on my list. Of bad things Saucy did."

"He bit Mom," Jammer chimed in.

Grandma waved her hand like that was nothing. But then Grandma shocked the whole car by bursting into tears! "Oh, Saucy!"

CHAPTER TWENTY-TWO

FORTY-NINE THINGS

They were all zombies the rest of the day, except for Jammer, who got out of the car and went straight to the backyard to smash pucks even harder than usual. K.C. played an adventure video game that took place during the Civil War, but Becca could tell he wasn't really into it, because he wasn't shouting at the screen.

All Becca wanted to do was lie on her bed— her bed that she'd be sleeping on again for the first time in at least a month. She looked at the list of forty-nine bad things. None of them were really all *that* bad. Except for the biting. But, like, they didn't really need living room curtains. Right? It was much nicer to have all the sunshine pouring in. As far as the screen door . . . well, that one was kind of bad, because they didn't really want flies getting into the house. On the other hand, a few flies never killed anyone. And what doesn't kill you makes you stronger. Why couldn't they just get some fly swatters?

Becca spent a lot of time thinking about each item, and whether it was really important or not. And most of them weren't. Which was starting to make her feel kind of outraged! Saucy did break the leg off one of the kitchen chairs, and Mom said she couldn't find a matching chair anymore because they had been "discontinued," which meant they didn't make them anymore. But who even cared if one of the chairs didn't match? Why was that even important? For instance, had anyone ever said, "I'm not eating dinner tonight because my chair doesn't match"? No, no one had ever said that since the beginning of time, Becca was sure of it.

She couldn't, however, come up with even a single excuse for Saucy biting Mom. Not one. But then she thought, *The bite hardly broke skin!* Still, she remembered one of Dad's clichés: caught between a rock and a hard place. She wasn't sure, but it seemed like that cliché fit her life right now. The rock was Saucy, and what a good and wonderful pig she truly was. The hard place was that Becca did not want anything or anybody biting Mom. She didn't want that at all.

After dinner, which was pizza that Mom ordered to make them all feel better, Becca didn't feel like being in the living room talking with them like they sometimes did, and she didn't feel like going for a walk with them, which they almost always did. Instead she went straight to bed without even brushing her teeth. That's right, she just went straight to bed with her dirty teeth. Which she never did, because she didn't like dirty teeth. But her parents always told them, *every single night*, to brush their teeth. Today, she wanted to show that she didn't care what they told her. She was mad at them! She might even hate them! She also started to think, *Even if the police had come for Saucy, why couldn't her parents just stick up for her?* Yes, she had panicked when she saw the factory farm, but now she saw that maybe she had overreacted. And, she decided, it was all her parents' fault!

Unfortunately, Becca found she did not even like her bed anymore. It was too soft. It was better to be lying on the kitchen floor with a pig. It was much, much better. She thought about how much better it was, and she started sobbing. Her brothers came in and got in bed too. Bailey started sobbing as hard as Becca was. K.C. looked intensely worried. Even Jammer looked trauma-tized. She could see their faces because nobody had bothered to turn off the light.

At last Jammer got up and turned it off, but the Milky Way didn't come on, because it was on a timer, and it was too early.

She tried to picture Saucy, tried to think about how sweet a pig she was. But it was hard for her to concentrate on that. Now—without Saucy— she was only Becca . . . that was what she kept thinking. The phrase kept washing through her brain, back and forth like a wave: *I'm only Becca.* She even murmured it: "I'm only Becca." She called out to her brothers. Jammer and K.C. were quiet, but Bailey was doing this hiccupy thing he always did after he cried.

"Do you guys ever think stuff like 'I'm only Jammer'? Or 'I'm only K.C.'? Or 'I'm only Bailey'?"

"Huh?" Jammer answered.

"No, I haven't ever thought that at all," Bailey said. *Hiccup.*

K.C. took a moment, then asked, "Do you mean 'only me' in the context of what a big universe this is, or seems to be?"

She wasn't actually sure what she meant, so she didn't know what more to say. Her brothers returned to their phones. Yet the thought kept swirling and swirling through her brain: *I'm only Becca.* Also: *My pig is gone.*

And as long as she was feeling sorry for herself, she also had another thought: *I don't even have a best human friend.*

I'm only Becca and my pig is gone and I don't have a best friend.

Now she felt triple terrible. Then she had a thought that miraculously managed to make her feel even worse. Had MacKenzie felt as bad when her mother was jailed as Becca did now? Had she thought, *I'm only MacKenzie and my mother is in jail and I don't have a best friend?*

Becca tried to focus really hard on her thoughts. Her ripped-up zafu was beside her on the bed, like the stuffed-animal dachshund called Black Doggie that she used to have when she was six, that she used to hug every night. She hugged the zafu to her; maybe it would help her concentrate. She thought, *It's weird because . . . because I think I could have stopped MacKenzie's family from moving away, even though I'm ONLY BECCA.* She could have. And she hadn't. She thought about Saucy, alone on the road before they found her. Before *Becca* had found her. *I was her hero, I was.*

Suddenly she sat straight up and reached for her phone, but she reached so fast that she accidentally slapped it to the floor, and fell off her bed reaching for it.

Jammer said, "What? Oh, it's only Becca."

She ignored him but sent a group text to her brothers. And heard their phones ding.

Lets go to factory farm lets see whats there. K?

Bailey answered first: *K*

K.C. texted: *Y?*

I wanna, she texted him. *R u with me?*

She looked up. Jammer had his earbuds in. His head was jerking to music as he stared at his phone. He looked the way he looked when he was getting hyped up for a game. Then Becca got his text: *K*

She closed her eyes, satisfied. She knew if they all did it, K.C. would come, just because he was one of them. Excitement surged through her, like her insides were filled with ice one moment, then filled with fire the next. But no more goo.

CHAPTER TWENTY-THREE

HOW SAUCY LIVED

Becca was lying quietly, her phone off, as the door opened. Her brothers must have been doing the same, because she heard Mom say, "They're asleep already, poor things."

Dad replied, "It's been a hard day. But it will make them stronger as they grow up and face the future."

And Becca knew he really, truly believed that. Because he said it, and he only said what he meant.

Mom groaned. "Oh, what a day. I need to go to bed myself." She closed the door.

Becca lay still as could be. She didn't move at all, did not do anything but think about Saucy, and what they were about to do, until what felt like an hour had gone by. Then Bailey said, "How about now?"

So they all got up and dressed, Bailey crawling to the bureau where his clothes were kept. K.C. looked doubtful. "Should we bring anything?"

"Like what?" Becca whispered.

He shrugged. "Dunno . . . a hockey stick, for protection?"

"Protection from what?" Jammer asked.

"I don't know. How about flashlights?"

"We have flashlights on our phones," Becca reminded him.

K.C. seemed deep in thought. "Never mind. I guess . . . I guess I'm just nervous. But you know what? I can do this."

Jammer lifted Bailey, saying, "Lemme carry you to the garage." That was where they kept his excellent wheelchair.

"Thanks, bud," Bailey said.

"All good, bud."

When Bailey was in his chair and they were all outside, Jammer stood for a moment with his eyes closed tight. Just like he had one time when he found out his teammate needed to go through chemo. Like he had so much emotion in him he couldn't stand it. Then he opened his eyes and said dramatically, "Let's do this."

The night was not warm and not cool. Muggy, but with a soft wind that seemed to blow the mugginess out of the way.

Though they walked as quietly as they could, Becca could hear their footsteps on the sidewalk, as well as the whir of Bailey's wheelchair motor. She glanced uneasily at the houses they passed, hoping nobody could hear those footsteps, that whir. When they got to the next road, there were no sidewalks, so they traveled on the shoulder.

The streetlights ended as they reached the out-skirts of town. Becca felt like she was in the wild, because at that moment the world seemed untamed and unpredictable. Like anything at all could happen, but not in a good way. For a moment, she debated turning back. But those nine long, windowless buildings . . . they were calling her. It was almost as if she didn't have a choice but to go see what they held.

When they reached the road that led to the factory farm, K.C. said, "I think I can do this, right?" He moved to the front of them all and walked firmly.

"Dude, do you want me to go in front?" Jammer asked.

"Nah, I'm good."

Jammer swaggered, like he always did. Bailey's head was tilted slightly, the way it was sometimes when he was thinking. "I love the sound of my chair," he said. For no reason.

Becca's legs felt robotic, not quite attached to her. She thought about how they had walked this road with Saucy just last night, when the world was a totally different place than it was tonight. Last night she still had a pig. Her life was completely different now, and yet everything in the world looked the same as it had yesterday.

"We're almost there," Bailey said quietly.

Becca understood instantly how he knew this: he had felt the warmth.

Jammer was the first to recognize the exact spot, maybe because he was the one who'd covered it up. He moved away the brush, made the hole even bigger for Bailey, and stepped through. Becca pushed Bailey after him, K.C. following.

It was as if they had entered a complete other universe. The air—it was totally different air they were breathing in here! It seemed like that, anyway. It was warmer, muggier. About a mile away, the nine long buildings appeared deserted. A body of water near the buildings looked like some kind of man-made lake, dark and shimmering under the moon. There was a sense almost of *nothingness* over there. Like not *evil*, which was kind of what she'd expected, but more like something unreal that was not a natural part of the rest of the world. Like . . . if you went on Google Maps and saw an image of a desert, and then in the middle of the desert were the nine buildings. There didn't seem to be any life anywhere, let alone thousands of pigs. The few lights were sickly and orangish.

Becca wavered, unsure whether they should just turn around and leave. But the buildings pulled her to them. And—and she wanted to see where Saucy had come from, how she had lived before they found her. Still . . . she wavered.

"We can do this," K.C. muttered. "Let's find out where Saucy came from."

"I think that's important," Bailey added.

Yet nobody moved. Becca willed herself to place one foot in front of the other. But it seemed that she had no will at all.

So she tried to scrape together all the focus and concentration she had inside of her. Then said firmly, *"Come on."*

They crossed the long, long field. It was full of ruts, but Bailey's wheelchair bounced right over them. An awful smell wafted toward them as they drew closer to the buildings. Or maybe the smell was coming from the lake? Wherever it came from, it made her feel nauseous. Bailey retched, spat a couple of times, and then immediately said, "Don't worry, I'm fine."

"You sure, bro?" Jammer asked.

"I said I'm fine," Bailey said firmly.

A sudden wind blew, cleared the air around them. "The simulation!" K.C. said excitedly. "It's on our side!"

Instead of thinking *whatever* like she usually did, Becca hoped he was right. When they reached the first building, she strode up to the door. It was metal and plain. She gazed up at the night sky and prayed softly, "Please don't let us get caught."

K.C. glanced at the sky and said, "We're going in."

Then Becca turned the knob.

CHAPTER TWENTY-FOUR

THE FACTORY FARM

So. Basically. The inside was one long room with an aisle down the middle, and on either side were metal enclosures, kind of like cages, a single bare lightbulb dangling above each. Each held a mother pig and a bunch of piglets. It looked like hundreds of little Saucys, some of them lying or standing in pee and poop, and some of them clean. The mothers were huge— Becca gasped at how huge they were. Saucy would be that size one day! Many were lying down, heaving on their sides. The enclosures were divided into two parts, one for the babies, and one for the heaving moms. The mothers'

enclosures were only big enough for them to lie or stand in, although some seemed unable to stand. The babies could fit through the bars to get milk from their moms. One mother was trying to reach for a baby pig who appeared to be sick, but she couldn't quite reach. Becca knew instantly that the mothers were in pure misery. You could feel the misery, filling the long room like something you could touch.

She heard one of her brothers throw up. But she couldn't tear her eyes away from the pigs to see who it was. It had seemed at the sanctuary that there were So. Many. Pigs. But this—this was a whole other level.

Finally she turned to check on her brothers. Jammer was staring at a mother who was standing, chewing emotionlessly on a metal bar in her little jail. Her gums were bleeding. Bailey was leaning all the way back in his chair, as if to get away, his eyes on a baby that was trying to stand up, but kept falling down.

K.C. was leaning over on his knees—he was the one who'd thrown up.

Even though there was squealing and grunting coming from all over, it wasn't as loud as you would have thought it would be with so many pigs. In fact, it seemed disturbing that it wasn't louder, more full of life.

But it was so hard to breathe! Becca started coughing, over and over. She felt like she might be choking. K.C. roused himself and said, "What are we doing here? I'm just wondering, Beccers, what are we doing?"

What *were* they doing?

But first she had to know: "K.C.? Is it—a simulation?"

"I—I—it doesn't matter," he replied.

Then Bailey began motoring himself forward. Becca followed him, down the middle of the long aisle, pigs on either side. Miserable pigs. The room seemed endless. Becca turned to make sure Jammer and K.C. were following. Jammer was kneeling in front of one of the enclosures. He pushed his hair out of his face and leaned in, then waved Becca over. There were nine piglets inside. One of them was super skinny, as skinny as Saucy had been when they found her. With scared eyes. *So* scared. Of *them*.

Jammer croaked, "My mouth is so dry." He looked like he had forgotten all about hockey for the first time in forever and would never think about it again.

K.C. was shaking his head. "It doesn't matter," he said in disbelief.

Is there anything else in the entire world more horrible than this place? Becca wondered. How could Saucy have escaped? She wished all these piglets could escape. But where would they go? Could they just open all the enclosures and shoo them out into the field?

Jammer stood up abruptly. "We gotta save some," he said. He had been thinking just like her! The mother pig he stood in front of was panting, her eyes half open. Becca came up beside him, and knew why he was focusing on this group. The skinny piglet looked exactly, precisely like Saucy. That is, they all looked a lot like Saucy, but one of them looked *exactly* like her.

Becca eyed the one who looked like Saucy. She was going to save that one *for sure*. But the one beside it, who didn't look so exactly like Saucy, touched Becca's heart by the way it blinked at her so innocently. Not an impertinent pig at all! She instantly loved them both!

"We could just set them all free?" Becca suggested.

"Wouldn't they just catch them again?" Bailey asked.

But they had to do something! Becca knew this. And from somewhere deep inside of her, courage started welling up. "Do you think we can get the mama on her feet? Get her to walk? And then take her and her piglets home?" She turned to Jammer hopefully. "You're strong. Can you lift her?"

"Becca, that pig has to weigh six hundred pounds." But then determination washed over his face. She had seen him do stuff in the last seconds of games. All the way in the stands, she had felt his determination to score, even if there were only ten seconds left.

Now, he fiddled unsuccessfully with the gate, then, exasperated, just climbed over the railing. He squeezed into the enclosure, stretched his arms around the big sow. And heaved. "Ahhhh!"

he grunted. His face scrunched up and turned red. Then deeper red. Becca willed him to be stronger. The sow seemed to have a slight bit of hope in her face! Jammer was grunting, then making a strange noise almost like a scraping sound in his throat. But he couldn't budge the sow.

He dropped his arms and seemed like he wanted to collapse, but there wasn't enough space. Instead he leaned his head back and stared at the ceiling. "I'm sorry," he said. "I'm so sorry." To the sow? To Becca?

He was crying.

Becca looked at her brother's sweaty face. Jammer was the one, really. He was the one who went out into the world and *did* things. He was not a thoughtful kid, not like Becca, Bailey, and K.C. She did not think he'd ever had a deep thought in his life. But he *did* things. And suddenly she *got* that.

She climbed over the railing herself. "We're taking the babies! *Now!*" she ordered. She picked up the one who'd looked innocently at her and handed it to K.C. Jammer immediately stopped crying and picked up the one who looked exactly like Saucy and laid it in Bailey's lap. The piglets were squealing, and this started a chain reaction. Soon other pigs were squealing throughout the room. It was growing insanely noisy.

"Give me another!" Bailey demanded, and Becca did. She kept passing the piglets to her brothers until they each had two. Becca dropped her two in Bailey's lap and climbed out, even though there was one left. But they couldn't hold any more.

Yet once she climbed out, she couldn't bear it. The one that was left was looking at her like it understood what was happening. That it was being left behind.

Bailey must have noticed because he said urgently, "I'll take three."

K.C. looked wildly around. "You can't hold three! Plus, what about all the others?" Then he added even more wildly, "Logic! We have to be logical! We can't save them all, you know!" But *then* he said, "Oh, *crap*," and suddenly set his piglets on the ground, climbed back in, and handed the extra one to Bailey.

Becca turned to the sow, saw understanding in her eyes. The sow grunted. She *knew* what they were doing. "I promise they'll have good lives," Becca told her.

As he climbed out of the enclosure, K.C. was murmuring, "Oh, crap. Oh, crap." And kind of hyperventilating.

But it was time to go.

"Come on!" Becca urged her brothers as K.C. picked up his two piglets. "Are you sure you can manage three, Bailey?" She took her two from his lap.

Bailey maneuvered his wheelchair toward the door, saying with outrage, "Of course I can! Don't wait up for me, just run!"

But Becca did wait up for him, not leaving the building until he had gotten out the door. Jammer and K.C. were already halfway across the field, Jammer with his long strides and K.C. practically keeping up with his legs in high gear. Bailey's chair bumped easily over the terrain. Jammer turned back to check on them. Then, seemingly satisfied that they were fine, he ran even faster.

Out of the corner of her eye, Becca thought she saw a pile of abandoned piglets as she ran. One might have been moving. But she couldn't save more—she couldn't!

Even though the piglets were small—she'd tucked one under each arm—they were already feeling heavy. One was wiggling so much it was hard to hold on. "I'm saving you," she scolded. Her voice sounded slightly hysterical. She felt something behind her, but when she checked over her shoulder, the field was empty behind them. She kept running. It seemed as if she had been running a much longer time than it had taken to walk to the buildings. She was panting. Bailey passed her by, his face intense, alive. He was trying to control the squirming piglets and manage his controls at the same time.

"You okay?" she called out.

"I'm good," he said, a little annoyed. "Save your pigs!" She could see K.C. struggling as well—running with piglets in your arms was hard! Only Jammer was nearly at the bushes.

She tried to run faster, but it seemed like the more she tried to speed up, the harder it was. Now she was sure she heard yelling behind them.

She was falling behind. But . . . but she had to rest. Had to. She knelt down . . . and was positive she heard yelling.

She gazed at the squirmiest pig and felt love well up in her, giving her energy. And suddenly Jammer was standing there, taking the piglets from her. "You're almost there. *Run!*" he urged.

She rose up, and her legs began pounding on the ground.

She almost moaned when she saw the bushes in front of her. "We're there, we're home free," she told herself, panting. She was the last one through.

On the other side, the boys had their piglets on the ground. One was already wandering off, but Jam grabbed it. K.C. was kneeling, breathing raspily. He and Becca caught eyes for a moment, and they smiled before getting super serious again. The special innocent piglet started

squealing as Becca picked it up. She cuddled it until it quieted down to a few whimpers.

After they'd all caught their breath, they turned toward home, silently, calmly walking along the road, hugging the shoulder. Quickly, too. But without running. A car passed by but didn't pay them any attention, or didn't seem to. As if seeing four kids with nine piglets this late at night was perfectly normal. They turned down a side road where there would probably be no traffic and continued on, the only sound Bailey cooing, "Shhhh, we're saving you. Shhhh." Sirens sounded somewhere. Maybe police coming for them. Probably for them.

They went down so many side roads that Becca wondered if they were lost. But then she saw a street she recognized.

Once home, they went straight into the backyard. Becca looked worriedly at the latch on the gate. She wished it had a lock! They tried to be very quiet. But there was some squealing. The piglet that looked like Saucy acted like her too! It looked demandingly at Becca and *barked*! All of a sudden Mom, in her pajamas, was in the doorway, saying, "What have you *done*?"

There was a silence, and then Bailey said, "We found some pigs, Mom."

Mom rubbed at her eyes with her palms. She stared at nine little pigs scampering on the concrete. Rubbed her eyes again. And finally asked, "In the same place where Saucy was?"

"Sort of," he said. "I mean, do you mean the exact same place, or sort of the same place?"

Instead of answering Bailey, however, Mom turned to Becca. "Becca, this is you! This is all you! You didn't just take them from that farm, did you? You didn't just trespass, did you? Well, you did. I know you did."

"It's not a farm, Mom!" Becca cried out. "It's a torture chamber."

Mom looked extremely concerned. Very, *very* concerned. *Super* concerned. About either the trespassing, or about the piglets. Maybe both?

Becca looked to Bailey for backup, but it was Jammer who spoke up. "It was torture, Mom," he said. "I mean, bruh . . ." "Bruh" spoken a certain way was what Jammer said sometimes when he meant *wow, brother*.

"Mom. Mom!" Becca said. "These pigs are being literally tortured on purpose. We rescued them!"

"We're heroes!" Bailey exclaimed.

"Mom, they live in their own poop," Becca added. "They hardly have any space. Some are half-dead. Mom, you have to see! Come with us, we'll show you!"

"Honey, you can't just rescue pigs from a

farm, no matter how bad it is. That's stealing. And trespassing." But she had squatted and was petting a piglet's ear. "This one looks like Saucy."

"They *all* look like Saucy," K.C. said. "But that one the most. Mom. Mom, when I saw all those pigs, at first I didn't get it, but as I was running away, saving my pigs, I could tell it was a simulation, but I realized we also have free will within the simulation. And if we have free will, it doesn't matter if it's a simulation. It matters a lot, but it also doesn't."

Everyone just looked at K.C. Becca knew they were all thinking, *What?*

"I have pictures, Mom," Bailey said, and he took out his phone and showed Mom photos that Becca hadn't even realized he'd been taking. Mom stood up to look, picking up the piglet she'd been petting. Becca looked too.

They were photos of everything they had just

seen in the whole long, windowless, unhappy room. As well as a close-up of a piglet looking at the camera, the pink eyelashes visible. It was hard to explain that piglet's expression. It was kind of blank, but also kind of expectant, like, *What's next? What new misery could be next?*

Mom pressed her lips together as she studied the pictures. She blinked away tears.

Victory! Mom was on their side now!

Becca rushed off then and found an eye-dropper, a turkey baster, leftover pellets, and some avocado. She began to drip water into the piglets' mouths, as did K.C., and they drank and drank like the water made them feel crazy. Bailey dropped himself to the grass and fed pigs pellets. Jammer gave them mashed avocado. K.C. held one to his chest and said, "I wish you could be my pig."

Mom stood with her hands on her hips,

muttering to herself like she did when the schedule in her head got temporarily jumbled, and she had to un-jumble it. She took a big breath. Then, hopefully, she said, "Maybe the local newspaper would be interested? The conditions *are* inhumane. That can't be legal . . . but it probably is."

K.C. looked surprised. "Mom, no! We don't know whose side the newspaper will be on."

"Nobody even reads the newspaper," Jammer said. That was probably true. Becca always saw the rolled-up local paper lying on people's driveways until garbage day.

"NO!" K.C. was shouting.

"Shhhh," Bailey said. Then he whispered, "Remember, we have stolen pigs here. I mean they're rescued, not stolen, but they're kind of stolen, too. But they're more rescued than stolen."

Then nobody talked. Becca tried to think

about what they could do. She picked up a piggy and held it to her like K.C. was doing with his. The cuteness was epic. She wanted to rescue *every* pig in that factory farm.

"You smell bad," she said to the pig, but she kissed it anyway. Admittedly, she did have a moment of wondering what would happen if her lips got mange.

Everybody fell silent for no particular reason. Then Becca had a thought. "How about we print out the pictures?" she said. "We'll post them on lampposts!"

"There's a problem with that. They'll get the security footage of us hanging up the pictures, and we'll be in trouble," K.C. argued. "Mom and Dad will have to pay a fine or something." He thought a moment. "We need to print out the pictures, and . . . and we can give them to all our friends, and *all* of us together will hang them on lampposts! We'll get all our classmates! All the hockey players! All the multiples we know! Every single kid! They can't fine all of us!"

Bailey looked up from the piglet he was feeding. "And the caption on the pictures should say, 'This is happening in *your* hometown.'"

CHAPTER TWENTY-FIVE

A MOMENT OF PEACE

Becca could tell Mom and her brothers were getting sleepy. In fact, while Jammer was feeding a piglet, his eyes closed and his head bobbed. Mom must have seen too, because she said, "What are you planning to do about sleep tonight?"

They decided to sleep with the pigs in the kitchen. So Becca and her brothers lay in their sleeping bags, the piglets nestling into a single pile on the psychedelic bed. At one point as everybody was settling in, Dad walked into the kitchen, stared for a minute with his mouth hanging open, said, "Okay, I'm dreaming," and returned to bed. Grandma never woke up. She was an extremely deep sleeper—she needed a lot of sleep, in order to have energy for all the scolding she did.

It was two in the morning. The pigs settled down quickly, like getting rescued was exceedingly exhausting.

Becca was so glad to be lying on the floor again, and surrounded by pigs. Still, none of them was Saucy, and she remembered how amazing—no, how perfect—it had been when Saucy lived here. These pigs were perfect too, but again she had the thought that none of them was Saucy.

"Do you think the mother pig died?" Bailey asked solemnly.

"No," Becca answered. "But at least she knew her babies were safe."

"No," K.C. said. "She's going to live and have more piglets."

"Then we haven't changed anything," Jammer said. He paused. "I'm going to be too tired to skate tomorrow." He paused again. "But that's okay. 'Night."

CHAPTER TWENTY-SIX

HOUSE OF PIGS

So Saucy times nine was a *lot* to handle. Because Jammer still needed to skate, and go to PT. And Bailey still needed to go to *his* PT. And K.C. still needed time by himself, just to think and concentrate on his theories. And Mom still needed to schedule. And Dad still needed to go to work.

However, except for Dad, they spent the whole first day not doing any of their things, Jammer not skating, and K.C. not thinking about the simulation, and Bailey canceling a PT appointment for the only time ever when he wasn't sick. All they did was take care of the pigs. Becca now understood what the phrase "run ragged" meant. It meant you were nonstop busy and never thinking about yourself for even a second. Becca did think about how her parents used to say they needed many helpers when they brought their quadruplets home. The house was always filled with friends and relatives and sometimes even random volunteers from an Ohio multiples group. Now, everybody warmed up milk and held babies and sang to them and fed them. And cleaned up.

Cleaning up after the piglets was the thing that took longest, even though seven of them knew instinctively to use the backyard as their toilet.

Grandma spent the whole day following them around, glaring and scolding. She made them clean with bleach seven times!

The nine piglets were all different. Here were their personalities:

SAUCY

1. The one who most resembled Saucy liked to cock her head and look at you like she was always confused.

2. Another had a very bad temper!

3. Another was lazy and just liked to lie around.

4. Another sniffed constantly like he had a cold.

5. Another clearly had a sense of humor and liked to take things from your hand and run off with them.

6. Another loved the remnants of the zafu and barked at you if you came near it!

7. Another loved to dig and destroyed Mom's garden that she had replanted!

8. Another spun in circles the minute he saw an avocado.

9. And the last liked to charge back and forth across the yard, over and over, as if she was trying to beat her best time.

When Dad finally got home that first day, he came into the backyard and looked from the pigs to each of his kids. Then he said, "They look like they're full of energy, and you all look tired."

But Becca and her brothers were too exhausted to even answer.

By the second day, Becca was so drained, she felt like she was experiencing brain freeze. And she had not been able to visit

Saucy yet, which made her sob at night until she fell asleep. The piglets were very cute and very demanding! Becca could not even go to the bathroom without taking the innocent one with her, because he demanded it. He needed to be with Becca at every moment, or he cried. As a matter of fact, all nine of the piglets started following Becca around wherever she went. Dad took about a hundred pictures and videos of them trailing her and kept saying, "You'll thank me someday for taking these."

Still. She was tired. She could not keep this up.

One night, when her brothers were so wiped out they decided to sleep in their beds, Becca lay alone on the kitchen floor surrounded by the piglets. They couldn't sleep on the dog bed anymore, because it was in shreds.

It was ten thirty.

Her mom had already phoned the sanctuary

about the piglets. But as much as Becca loved having the piglets around, she couldn't sleep at all. Because she knew these piglets would be fine at the sanctuary, and she knew Saucy would be fine. But what about the hundreds of pigs she'd seen personally at the factory farm? And the thousands more that would have been living in the other long buildings? What about *them*? So before giving the Naughty Nine up, she and her brothers decided to call all the kids they knew to ask for help ridding their town of the factory farm. And they would invite the kids over to meet the piglets! Another donation would be necessary, Becca knew that, and then the pigs would be gone. She worried about how much this donation would have to be. Probably massive, if it meant for sure keeping the pigs safe forever. At least Jammer's skates weren't getting tight yet. And Bailey's wheelchair was still new.

It was true, though, that maybe Jammer would have to keep his skates longer, until his toes hurt quite a bit, and maybe he'd miss a few physical therapy sessions, because even though they were all equal, Bailey's therapy was the actual most important thing in their household. And quite possibly, the donation would have to be more of a promise than actual money, at least until the "tax refund" arrived magically one day. Or—or maybe Lady would decide she would take the piglets and care for them forever without a donation. If she could even make that decision by herself.

But anyway, the piglets were all around her, some of them snorting in their sleep. The whole house was slumbering except for her.

She loved these pigs a lot. And yet that night Becca felt lonely. For Saucy. Even for her brothers. She wished Saucy hadn't grown so fast. She wished her brothers were here sleeping with her. She wished she still had a best friend that she could share all this with. MacKenzie would have *loved* these pigs! Becca knew that, because she and MacKenzie were different people, yet they almost always loved the same things.

She felt her eyes fill with tears. How could you feel lonely surrounded by nine piglets you adored? And yet she did. Because they would be gone soon.

And suddenly she unlocked her phone and punched in MacKenzie's number. She felt all the cowardice in her soul flooding to the surface, making her hands shake so much that she punched in the wrong number three times. But the fourth time she got it right. She wanted to tell Mac a lot of things. Like for instance, everything that had happened with Saucy and the factory farm and these pigs breathing and snoring around her. And she had to say some other stuff that she couldn't even think about—she was just going to have to say it all without thinking.

It was nearly midnight, but still MacKenzie answered sleepily after the third ring.

"Becca?" she asked disbelievingly.

"Hi, MacKenzie."

There was a long pause before Mac answered, "Hi."

And with Becca lying there on the floor, missing Saucy, surrounded by baby pigs, feeling alone and yet not, it all poured out: "MacKenzie, I have a lot to tell you, about a pet pig I got who came from a factory farm, and about how I'm lying here now with nine baby pigs around me, and about, well, about how I'm really sorry I didn't stick up for you and stay your friend when your mom, you know, your mom—when she went away. You were always a best friend to me, and I wasn't a best friend back. I was a horrible person because I'm a scaredy-cat of a human being. I'm a better person with pigs, honestly, and I'm sorry." She took a breath. And burst into tears.

"I know," MacKenzie said simply. "My parents said you weren't sorry, but I knew you were." But she added a little harshly, "I didn't need you anyhow. I have a lot of friends from my new school."

Becca deserved that. She knew she did.

"I'm happy that you have a lot of friends," she replied quickly, and it was true. "And I just wondered, can we be friends too?"

MacKenzie cleared her throat as if she was going to make an announcement. Then her voice choked a little as she said, "I think so. My mom and dad might say no. But I—some people gave my mom a second chance, so I believe in that." She paused, then added excitedly, "What do you mean you have nine pigs?"

CHAPTER TWENTY-SEVEN

THE MEETING

Then Becca and her brothers did what they said they were going to do. While their mother piglet babysat, they spent two hours calling everyone they knew and managed to find a lot of kids who agreed to hang flyers of the inside of the farm on lampposts and telephone poles and to slip some under car windshield wipers. To be honest, Becca had had visions of more than a hundred kids. They ended up with forty-seven, which was actually extremely excellent, when you thought about it. First they would all meet at the house. Hockey boys, some multiples they knew, the girls who'd been mean to Mac but loved the pigs so now were less mean, a few neighbor kids, and Bailey's whole class. Plus the science kids who played Xbox with K.C.

When they were finished calling, they went out back and found Mom running up and down the yard panting, nine piglets chasing her as she laughed.

Becca and her brothers just watched, because Mom looked so happy. So did the pigs.

Oh, and MacKenzie. When Becca had told her about the big meeting with the kids, she said she wanted to come, even though some of them had been mean to her. Becca was totally surprised, but had mad respect. The pigs are more important than a bunch of kids, Mac said. She and Becca had talked for three hours on the phone, until Becca could hardly keep her eyes open, so Becca knew they could—and would— be best friends again. "I have a million friends now," MacKenzie kept saying. "I'm the best girl volleyball player *and* girl basketball player at my school *and* the best baseball player, girl or boy." Mad respect.

MacKenzie came early, before anyone else. She'd grown at least four inches, and she seemed confident and nervous at the same time. Then just nervous, until Becca took her into the backyard to see the piglets. Then MacKenzie fell to her knees and opened up her arms and said excitedly, "Come, please come!" And one of them did, the innocent one. MacKenzie scooped him up, and suddenly she was crying.

She pushed her face into the piglet, who Becca had named Henry, and blurted out, "I have two sort-of friends, and I'm a good volleyball player but not the best, and I don't play basketball or baseball at all."

Becca blurted out, "I only have my pig, Saucy. She's my best friend!"

And then they were both crying a little, and hugging the pigs a little, and then the doorbell was ringing.

They had never had so many kids at their house before! And some parents stayed instead of dropping their kids off. The hockey boys were out of control!

The kids kept saying, "Bring the pigs inside! Please bring the pigs inside!" So Becca did, without asking her parents, because she wanted to make sure to please all these kids who were hopefully going to save thousands of piglets from torture. But the house was so noisy and crowded that the piglets got upset and began charging at some of the kids, as if they were giants instead of tiny fifteen-pounders. K.C. took the piglets back outside to calm down, a trail of friends following him.

Becca glanced around the room and spotted MacKenzie talking to *Jammer*. And Jammer was talking back. It looked like he was speaking in whole sentences and even *paragraphs*. To someone who didn't even play hockey!

Dad came home with ten boxes of pizzas, and those outside came in, and everybody fell upon the boxes like they were starving.

Bailey got so excited by all the commotion that he raised a fist in the air. "Pig liberation!" he shouted. Everybody cheered and raised their fists in the air as if they were freedom fighters!

And suddenly Becca noticed that MacKenzie's mom was there, standing off by herself. Mac had come to the door alone earlier. Had her mom just been sitting in the car?

Becca got a sickly feeling in her stomach.

But. This experience would be part of the new Becca, the Becca who was saving thousands of pigs, hopefully. The new, brave Becca. The good-person Becca. She had already decided yesterday what she would say if one of MacKenzie's parents came to the house. So she walked over to Mrs. Fulton.

"Umm," she said. That actually wasn't what she'd planned to say! For a second she forgot what was next.

Mrs. Fulton was looking at her guardedly, even suspiciously.

"It's . . . very nice to see you, Mrs. Fulton," Becca blurted out, remembering. "I sincerely hope you're doing very well." It had taken her an hour to come up with that, but as she said it, she knew it wasn't nearly enough. So she added, "I mean truly sincerely." That still seemed inadequate, but she couldn't think what else to say. So she hugged Mrs. Fulton instead and just exclaimed, "I'm sorry I was mean to MacKenzie!"

Mrs. Fulton hesitated, her arms hanging limply, then at last hugged Becca back. "You're a nice girl, I know you are." But she said it as if maybe she'd had some doubts previously.

Becca tried to think of what more to say, but MacKenzie and Jammer had walked up, and Mac exclaimed, "Jammer still plays hockey, and I told him that one time, when we visited Minnesota when I was nine, I saw a hockey game."

And then Jammer and Mac started talking to each other *more*, even though Jammer never talked to girls unless it was to say things like "You're in the way" or "What?" or "Yeah." Sometimes he also said, "Whatever." In fact, mostly he said, "Whatever." But he was speaking in *whole sentences* to MacKenzie, and MacKenzie was totally ignoring Becca. Which didn't seem right.

"Yeah, I play a game every week, except for tournaments, when I play four games on the weekends," he was saying.

"I love tournaments!" MacKenzie said excitedly. "We have them in volleyball, too, and my team won the last two I got to play in!"

And they kept talking, and kept ignoring Becca. That was just . . . just *wow*, Jammer, *wow*. But Becca had to admit it made her feel happy when she saw how lit-up their eyes were. She *wanted* to contribute to MacKenzie feeling happy, even though what she was contributing was her brother. Jammer offered to show MacKenzie his sweaty hockey gear as proudly as Becca might have offered to show somebody Saucy! He didn't say it was sweaty, but Becca knew it was. It smelled bad—that was why it was only allowed in the garage.

Grandma was frowning at them from across

the room. But then she turned to the room in general and frowned at all of them. Next she walked right up to Becca and frowned. "All this commotion over some pigs!" she cried out. She was still standing in front of Becca, but she was looking up as if she was complaining to the ceiling. Which was something new from Grandma, but somehow not surprising. But Becca knew that Grandma really liked the pigs, because yesterday she'd spent the afternoon in the backyard with them. Becca and her brothers had peered out a few times to see what she was doing.

At first Grandma sat in a lawn chair, surrounded by piglets she was feeding melon chunks to. Then she started walking back and forth across the yard with her bag of melon. The piglets followed her, grunting and snorting excitedly every time she handed one a piece of fruit. She would walk in one direction, then abruptly turn around, as if she really enjoyed them abruptly turning with her. It was her little army, like she secretly wished she was a general. General Grandma.

MacKenzie was squinting at the section of the ceiling that Grandma was complaining to. "I don't think she's actually looking at anything special," Becca explained.

"She's just Grandma," Jammer explained further. "I mean, you can't really try to figure it out, you know? But, hey, lemme show you my gear."

Then Jammer and MacKenzie walked off to the garage. *WOW*, Jammer.

After the pizza was devoured, Becca brought kids out back in groups of five to meet the piglets in a more personal fashion. They all oohed and aahed and *loved* them so much. Becca had a whole little presentation she had memorized about how bad factory farms were, but since she'd already told them all this on the phone, she could see everybody's eyes glaze over. It dawned on her that whenever she memorized anything she planned to say, it always sounded boring when she actually said the words out loud to someone. So probably she would need to cut "speechwriter" off her list of future jobs she could do someday when Jammer was a hockey player, K.C. was a scientist, and Bailey was a songwriter.

K.C. had printed out color flyers with Bailey's pictures from the factory farm. On the bottom in his shaky handwriting, Bailey had put their initials: BBKCJ. Just because even though all the kids were now in this together, the four of them were the ones who had started it. According to Bailey, the first B stood for Becca.

Each group of kids would be working as a team. They took piles of flyers to hang up on lampposts, starting the next day. That way, they wouldn't all be leaving this house together and immediately go hang the flyers, which K.C. said everyone in the neighborhood would notice and would somehow cause Mom and Dad to be fined ten thousand dollars. Or maybe less. He wasn't exactly sure. In any case, it was a way of beating the simulation. Or something.

And Jammer and MacKenzie were in the garage the *whole* time. Wow . . .

CHAPTER TWENTY-EIGHT

TRANSCENDING

So then. At exactly one p.m. the next day, groups of several kids each began hanging flyers on lampposts, store bulletin boards, and telephone poles. They went into parking lots and placed flyers under windshields. They were *warriors*. And the effect was immediate. Becca could see that. She saw people pick up the flyers and stare with surprise and horror at the pictures. They were *horrified* at what was happening in their own town. Their ordinary little town.

And all of this occurred because an impertinent, mangy, somewhat demanding factory-farm piglet had somehow managed to make her way to the side of the road.

Becca spent the rest of the day swaggering like a hockey boy. They all did.

But the other thing: Mom had made arrangements to take the piglets to the sanctuary that very afternoon. So when the flyers were hung, Becca's family piled the piglets into the van. And, and, Jammer—he'd invited MacKenzie to meet them there. The *wow*s just kept coming. Mr. Fulton was going to bring her, probably to see if he approved of Jammer.

The piglets scampered around the van floor. Becca would miss them! She tried to remember: Was there a word that meant happy and sad at the same time?

Then K.C. looked up from his phone and said, "*Saudade.*" And Becca knew exactly what he was trying to say. Because the simulation. He continued, "I was just looking up words for how I feel, and I found this Portuguese word, *saudade*. It means 'the pleasure I suffer.'"

Jammer gazed at him, nodding. Then he said, "That's actually deep."

K.C. looked a little surprised and a little pleased, because, Becca knew, nobody ever told K.C. he was deep. Even though he was.

At the sanctuary, they each carried a pair of piglets out of the car. Mom carried the ninth one, with Grandma complaining, "Why don't I get a pig?" Then when Becca tried to hand her one, she said, "Never mind, nobody cares about me!"

As soon as they all stepped inside the gate, and the piglets were loose, they fanned out snorting and running, and Becca could just *feel* that this was the actual best moment of their lives. Henry stopped running, let out a long, loud snort, and started running again.

Meanwhile Saucy, who looked bigger than

she had a few days ago, was barreling so hard toward Becca that Becca wondered if she would get bowled over. And she did, falling into a mud puddle. Then Saucy suddenly decided she was angry at Becca, probably because Becca hadn't had a chance to visit. Saucy literally stuck her snout into the air, walked up to K.C., and began cuddling with him, glancing over once to see if Becca was watching. Which she was.

But a minute later, Saucy came back, and Becca's family and all the pigs sat in the grass together eating fruit and carrots. Saucy ate about ten times more than any of them did.

When Mac showed up, she and Jammer didn't seem all that interested in the pigs. As Mr. Fulton looked on from a few yards away, with his arms crossed, Mac and Jammer stood right next to a sow talking about how sometimes you think you're hitting the puck or volleyball just right,

and then you whiff. It seemed a little strange for them to be standing in the middle of all these adorable pigs and talking about sports, but then Becca had never had a boyfriend, so what did she know?

The sanctuary seemed like a very good place. Becca was feeling rather satisfied with herself. The *only* problem was she still had her list of forty-nine items Saucy destroyed. But someday she would make up every single thing she had to make up in the world. She had already started. For instance, she and MacKenzie had become friends again. And she was going to replant the garden, and she was going to save her Christmas money and allowance for new living room curtains. Even though as it turned out, the curtains had been kind of expensive, because they were custom-made and they had come with the house when they bought it. So that one might take time.

Saucy had trotted off, and the little pigs had gathered around her in a circle. Not like Saucy was their mom. More as if Saucy was their *queen*. And she had a look on her face like, *Yes, yes, I am Queen Saucy*.

Then all ten pigs came over suddenly to sniff at Becca's backpack. Saucy lay against her for a couple of minutes before starting to push her nose at the backpack. She started biting it! Then she picked up Becca's backpack and ran off. Becca chased her. "Saucy, stop! Saucy!" She thought about what Bailey had suggested and called out, "Saucy, it's all your idea to stop! You *want* to stop!" But Saucy didn't. Want to, that is.

By the time Becca caught up, the backpack was ripped open, and Saucy was chomping on the cabbage that had been inside, the little ones pushing each other to get at the cabbage as well. When they finished eating, one of the piglets barked at Becca in quite a demanding fashion. Even more demanding than Saucy had ever been.

"I don't have any more," Becca explained, but the piglet barked a few more times before running off for no apparent reason.

Becca picked up the remnants of her backpack, then looked out at the field full of pigs.

Her mind drifted back to that moment when she and her brothers had first stepped into the long building. It was as if their entire lives had fallen away, and the only things in the world were them and the sad, sad pigs. The sadness of the pigs transcended hockey; transcended songs; transcended the simulation. The only thing that mattered was this: *We need to do something*.

Becca leaned her head back, could feel a sudden cool drizzle on her face, could smell a musty piggy scent. Maybe Saucy would live another ten years. Maybe by then every factory farm in Ohio would be totally gone, and Becca would have had something to do with that. It was possible, wasn't it?

Even just six months ago, she had still been a bad person. She hoped that being a hero to pigs would make up for that, would make it right. You couldn't erase the things you had done wrong in life, but you *could* make them right.

And always, for the next ten years, even though Becca might go to college, even though she might get a job in another town, even though she might save a million other pigs, she would keep returning here, for as long as Saucy lived. Becca had taken her grandfather's advice and figured out a little early some things she had to do. As K.C. might say, that was just Grandpa, making his mark on the simulation.

Now, K.C. said to Becca, "I dunno. I just dunno.

I guess . . . I guess if the aliens are actually dead now, or maybe they're alive but have abandoned us, we're in charge of the simulation ourselves. And Saucy, all by herself, managed to change the whole simulation they programmed."

"Do you think?" Becca asked. She thought it was possible.

Because Saucy was a *queen*. In fact, right this moment she was rolling in some mud. Just like you would do if you were a queen . . . who also happened to be a pig.

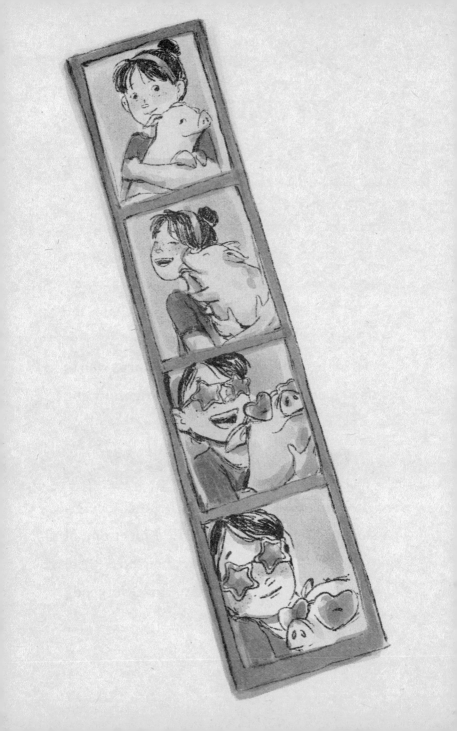

ACKNOWLEDGMENTS

As always, thanks to the extraordinary crew at Atheneum. I give thanks on the daily for my editor, Caitlyn Dlouhy, and publisher, Justin Chanda. Like, literally, every day I stop whatever I'm doing and take a moment to thank the heavens for them and for the faith that they've shown in me over the years. Thank you as well to managing editor Jeannie Ng: super-rigorous and yet sooooo nice! And to Audrey Gibbons—how is it that all these people can be so great at their jobs and so nice at the same time? Deepest thanks as well to Alex Borbolla and to the high-energy, passionate sales force. Every time I meet one of the sales people, I'm struck by their breadth of knowledge. They seem like they know everybody and everything.

I absolutely love Lauren Rille's jacket and book design—it fits the novel so exactly and brings a smile to my face every time I see it. And Marianna Raskin's illustrations are a force unto themselves.

Much, much, *much* appreciation to Jeff, Rhonda, Briana, Conor, Dillon, and Darian Rosenlieb—with the quadruplets listed in birth order! ☺) They were absolutely delightful to Skype with. And Rhonda has been open and fun and lovely and generous in taking the time to answer all my questions.

I can't even express how grateful I am to Brittany Sawyer, who runs an online group of pig "owners," many of whom are "owned" by their pigs. She so graciously helped me out by posting a questionnaire to her group, as well as answering the questions herself. And thank you to group members Elizabeth Birch, Alex Boring, Kathleen McKee, Michele Wardwell Nickell, Christina O'Sullivan, Deana Smallwood, Wendy Suto, as well as those who answered anonymously. The details provided by all of you were fun and funny and touching and emotional, and gave me so much insight into pigginess! I'm also extremely grateful to PETA and to Heidi Parker for all they do for animals and for corresponding with me about aspects of the story. Thank you especially to Heidi for passing the manuscript along for someone at PETA to read.

Finally, thanks to Meredith Turner-Smith for setting up my brief interview with Gene Baur, and to Gene for chatting about pigs.

READING GROUP GUIDE FOR

SAUCY

BY CYNTHIA KADOHATA

ABOUT THE BOOK

As the oldest in a set of quadruplets, Becca doesn't feel like she plays any special role in her family. One day, when her family is out for a walk, they find a sick, abandoned piglet by the side of the road. Becca convinces everyone that she can take care of her, and she names her piglet Saucy. Soon Saucy has taken over the family's hearts and household, but not without destruction and mayhem! As Saucy grows bigger and bigger, Becca must figure out what to do with her pig and how to stop her from destroying any more of the family home. What follows is a journey of discovery for Becca, both in learning more about herself and where Saucy came from. Filled with humor and engaging family dynamics, *Saucy* is a heartwarming story of the surprising friendship between a young girl and her pig.

DISCUSSION QUESTIONS

1. Becca's dad is famous for using clichés. For example, "being on cloud nine" or "a new lease on life." Why do you think he does this? In your reading journal, keep a list of the clichés Becca's dad uses and how they fit each moment of the story.

2. Becca is part of a set of quadruplets. Why is this important to the book's events? How does it affect

the way Becca views herself? What does Becca see as special about each of her siblings? What is special about Becca that she doesn't realize?

3. What does Becca mean when she says she's a jellyfish and her brothers are sharks?

4. Becca finds an abandoned little pig on a family walk and insists on keeping her as a pet. Why is this so important to her? What motivates her to keep the animal? Why does she name her Saucy?

5. As Saucy becomes a part of Becca's family, things start to go wrong. In fact, Becca has a list of forty-nine things that Saucy has ruined or done. Find three or four examples of the trouble Saucy has caused, then explain why these situations are problematic and how Becca might make it up to her family. Brainstorm ways she might do this without using money to pay her parents back.

6. When Becca leaves the veterinarian hospital, she offers to come back to visit the animals and help clean up. She's told that this is not necessary and that she should continue "just being [herself]." What does this statement mean to you? What do you think it means to Becca? Do you find it easy or challenging to "be yourself"? Does this change in certain situations?

7. Compare and contrast the care and feeding of a pig with a dog, cat, or other common household pet. Create a chart that shows the similarities and differences between food, housing needs, vet visits, and other costs.

8. Why does Becca feel a sense of peace when she is with Saucy? What makes you feel that way? Explain your answers.

9. Everything with Saucy seems to happen for a

reason. What is the significance of Saucy biting Mom in the garden? What happens after this?

10. The phrase "between a rock and a hard place" is another cliché. What is Becca's rock and hard place with Saucy? Can you think of a rock and a hard place for yourself?

11. Becca thinks, *I'm only Becca and my pig is gone and I don't have a best friend.* She's afraid to make new friends and thinks she's a coward for feeling this way. If you were her sibling, what advice would you give her? How would you help encourage her? Why can it be challenging to find confidence?

12. Do you think the family makes the right choice by giving Saucy to a sanctuary? Explain your answer. What would you have done if you were in their shoes?

13. Why is the last walk with Saucy so important for the family? What happens during that walk and later on as a result of this time together? Why is this an important moment for Becca?

14. Why do the kids sneak back out after their family walk? What is their plan? Do you agree or disagree with their decisions? Explain your answer. What other suggestions might you have for them about ways they can address their concerns?

15. How does the community react to the discovery of the pig farm and its treatment of pigs? How might you become involved if you heard about a similar situation in your area?

16. Becca is feeling terrible and sad about taking the piglets to the sanctuary. Her brother K.C. finds the Portuguese word *saudade*, which means

"the pleasure I suffer," to help them reflect and process. How does this word explain Becca's feelings and those of her brothers'? Why is this an important moment in the story?

17. The author, Cynthia Kadohata, interviewed a number of people who own or have worked with pigs extensively. The emotions Saucy displays reflect actual real-life details from real-life pig owners. Name some of these scenes and reactions in the text. What is Saucy doing during these moments? How do these occasions change or add to your understanding of Saucy or your perception of her situation? How can you tell if the animals in your life are feeling happy, afraid, or upset?

18. What do the illustrations add to the story? What do you learn from them? Think about experiencing a story through different mediums,

including how it might feel to listen to the audiobook of *Saucy*. How might hearing the character's voices rather than reading the words on a page change the way you feel about the story?

19. Name at least one other story in which a pig or another animal plays an important role. Compare and contrast these stories with *Saucy*. For example, consider using *Charlotte's Web*, *The Adventures of Nanny Piggins*, or books from the Mercy Watson series.

This guide has been provided by Simon & Schuster for classroom, library, and reading group use. It may be reproduced in its entirety or excerpted for these purposes.

Looking for another great book?
Find it
IN THE MIDDLE.

Fun, fantastic books for kids
in the in-be**TWEEN** age.

IntheMiddleBooks.com

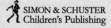

Don't miss any of these amazing novels from the winner of the National Book Award and the Newbery Medal,

CYNTHIA KADOHATA:

Pablo is the boy who washed up on the beach in a raft when he was a baby.

Birdy is the flightless parrot who washed up with him.

The islanders have kept Pablo and Birdy safe ever since, but the winds of change are blowing, and with them come myths of seafaring parrots that know all the words of the world, of fortunes gained and fortunes lost, and of a little dog, also lost . . .

Meet Bingo and Jmiah. They are going to save their beloved
Sugar Man Swamp from a gator wrestler determined to turn it
into an alligator-and-pony show and from a herd of feral hogs, and
they are going to discover art on the way. For they are Scouts.
They are best brothers. They are raccoons on a mission!

From Kathi Appelt, author of the Newbery Honor Book and
National Book Award finalist THE UNDERNEATH.

Caitlyn Dlouhy Books
atheneum Atheneum Books for Young Readers

PRINT AND EBOOK EDITIONS AVAILABLE • simonandschuster.com/kids